Tryggred by the ORC

AN MM MONSTER ROMANCE TALE

FINLEY FENN

Edited by Eris Adderly
Cover artwork by Skadior Art
Cover design by The Book Brander
Supported by the generous members of the Orc Sworn Patreon

~

Tryggred by the Orc

~

Sign up at www.finleyfenn.com for bonus stories and epilogues, delicious orc artwork, complete content guidance, news about upcoming books, and more!

ALSO BY FINLEY FENN

ORC SWORN

The Lady and the Orc

The Heiress and the Orc

The Librarian and the Orc

The Duchess and the Orc

The Midwife and the Orc

The Maid and the Orcs

The Governess and the Orc

The Beauty and the Orcs

The Widow and the Orcs

Offered by the Orc

Yuled by the Orcs

Tryggred by the Orc

ORC FORGED

The Sins of the Orc

The Fall of the Orc

THE MAGES

The Mage's Maid

The Mage's Match

The Mage's Master

The Mage's Groom

Written for my generous supporters and friends on Patreon.
Thank you.

AUTHOR'S NOTE

Greetings, dear reader!

Thank you so much for reading this MM Orc Sworn novella!

This book was first written for the generous members of my Orc Sworn Patreon, who wanted to learn how a swaggering Skai like Tryggr first fell for a shy sweetheart like Eben. Therefore, this book takes us slightly back in time, to the events of *The Maid and the Orcs* (the sixth full-length book in my Orc Sworn series).

But this time, we'll get to see the other side of the story, and find out what really went on behind the scenes! This means you will get multiple spoilers for *The Maid and the Orcs*—and while this story can still be read as a stand-alone, I think you'll appreciate it more if you've already read *The Maid and the Orcs*.

Also, this story does include some dark themes and situations, unhealthy dynamics, and very intense scenes. If you'd like full details on what to expect, please visit this book's page on my website at www.finleyfenn.com.

I really hope you have fun with *Tryggred by the Orc*! Hugs from Orc Mountain!

Yours,
Finley

1

The first time Eben caught sight of the tall, stunning Skai, said Skai was laughing, and grinding bollocks-deep into another orc's arse.

"Ach, you like that?" the Skai said, his voice hungry and low. "Wish for more?"

The bent-over orc—another Skai, by the scent of it—groaned and nodded, his claws dragging against the wall. And behind him, the tall orc laughed again as he drew himself out, slowly revealing a long, slick, heavily scarred prick. A prick that looked just as dangerous as the rest of him, what with his tall, muscled grey body, his long black claws, and his messy black topknot, with a gleaming steel *dagger* casually stabbed through it.

But he was still smiling down at the groaning orc, his dark eyes warm and approving, his claws slowly dragging down the orc's sides—and in a sharp snap of hips, he slammed back inside. Burying himself deep in one swift, stabbing stroke, while the orc yelped and shuddered upon him.

Eben shivered too, and his grip on the bottle of tonic in his hand had slackened, enough that it nearly dropped to the floor.

But he fumbled and caught it just in time, gripping it with shaky fingers, clutching it close to his wildly thudding heartbeat.

Foolish. Foolish, to notice such things. Foolish to care. He could have a good hard ploughing anytime he wished, and many of the orcs who frequented the Ka-esh *dýflissa* were just as commanding, just as handsome. And like most of the Ka-esh, this Skai was keeping to his own clan for his pleasures, for it was easier that way. Safer. Most of all when it came to Clan Skai.

Never trust a Skai, Eben's father had warned him again and again, all through the years of his youth. *Never let one touch you or find you alone. Instead you run as deep as you can, until you find a tunnel you can collapse behind you.*

Eben had studiously heeded the warning, and all the dark tales that had whispered and festered beneath it. Skai were greedy. Lawless. Reckless. Dangerous. And even now, so many summers after his father's passing, Eben still kept a careful distance—to the point where his boss Efterar, the mountain's Chief Healer, had needed to prod him to bring up this tonic to Dvergr, whose room was deep in the Skai wing.

You'll be perfectly safe, Efterar had said in his usual matter-of-fact way, giving a firm clasp of his hand to Eben's shoulder. *No Skai's going to look twice at you.*

Eben had nodded and obeyed, though the unease had kept twisting, tangling with something damnably like fear, as he'd quietly crept through the Skai wing, sniffing out Dvergr's distant scent. *Perfectly safe. No Skai's going to look twice at you.*

But now—Eben's breath caught as the tall, lean Skai laughed again, and ground in deeper—maybe Eben *wanted* a Skai to look at him. Wanted *this* Skai to look at him, with that easy, greedy grin, those warm, approving eyes. But those eyes were still fixed on the bent-over orc, and one of those clawed hands was digging into the orc's trembling flank, while the other hand gave a ringing little slap to his arse.

"More, sweet thing," the tall Skai ordered, husky but firm. "Know you can milk me harder than this, ach?"

The orc choked and nodded, his face contorting with palpable effort, and behind him the tall orc rasped out a low groan, his head tilting back. "Ach, that's good," he breathed, his hands stroking with obvious approval. "Don't stop."

The scent of his pleasure was now unfurling through the air, simmering sweet and heavy in Eben's nostrils. Strong enough to set his own prick stirring, the hunger coiling deep in his belly—and he flinched at the feel of it, jerked a hard shake of his head.

No. No. *Foolish*. The orc was Skai, reckless, dangerous, and openly fucking in the corridors was against the rules now, not that any Skai had ever seemed to notice. And—a sharp pang caught and twisted in Eben's chest as he watched the orc's stroking hands—maybe these orcs were... mated. Maybe the tall Skai was bound to the bent-over one. For as long as Eben could remember, Skai had refused to take other orcs as mates, or even offer them fidelity—until a few moons before, when the Skai had finally come together to alter their customs and recognize such bonds. And this tall, stunning Skai could have his choice of mates, could he not? Could pick from any number of eager worshippers, willing to bend and kneel, and offer him the fealty he deserved...

Foolish, *foolish*, and Eben squeezed his eyes shut, and forced himself to move again. To step that way, over there, toward Dvergr's distant scent, away...

"Looking for something, Ka-esh?" cut in a voice, and Eben gasped and startled, whipped around to where the tall Skai was—looking at him. Looking at him, oh, his brow creasing, even as he kept grinding into the other orc's upraised rump. "Not lost, are you?"

Eben nearly dropped the tonic again, but he clutched it closer against his chest, and desperately fought to find his voice. "I am seeking—Dvergr," he said, in a cracked, croaking whisper. "Wish to give him—tonic. Medicine. From the sickroom."

He winced even as he spoke, shaking his head, because curse him, from where else could the tonic have come—but the tall orc's mouth drew into a smile again, quick and easy and approving. "Ach, I see," he replied, with a sideways jerk of his dagger-adorned head. "Good of you to bring it. An' he's just down that way, ach? Keep turning left, you can't miss him."

Right. Eben rapidly nodded, too hard and urgent, but his feet seemed frozen in place, his eyes fixed on the orc's face. On that warm, genial smile, so stunning, so approving. And not fading even a little as Eben kept standing there staring, his face flooding with heat and shame and longing...

"Just come back if you get lost," the orc's voice continued, as his clawed hands spread wider against the orc's hips, his own hips moving more leisurely now, his fat, scarred, dripping length slipping in and out with brazen, astonishing ease. "I can show you the way, ach?"

Oh. Oh, fuck. And the orc even winked at Eben—*winked*, at him!—as he kept sliding in and out of the other orc's rump. As if he wanted Eben to look, as if he liked him looking, liked making him hot and flustered and—

And miserable. Miserable, or even despairing, because there was no way. No way something like this would ever end well. No way this Skai wouldn't crush Eben underfoot, and leave him ruined and empty.

Never trust a Skai. Never let one touch you, or get you alone...

And with a jolt, a flinch, a frantic gulp from his throat, Eben spun around, and fled.

2

Eben spent the evening bent over and begging in the Ka-esh *dýflissa*, taking his relief however he could gain it.

There was never a shortage of options in the clan's dark, well-equipped pleasure-room, most of all for an unmarked, unmated, eager young Ka-esh with no limits or boundaries. Eben was more than happy to bend, to beg, to bleed, to welcome whatever pricks might wish to use him, no matter the orc or the clan in question. And while Skai orcs still never came to the *dýflissa*—Eben had heard they had their own dedicated pleasure-room, deep in that Skai wing—these days there was usually a big, brawny Ash-Kai or two, and occasionally an adventurous, fat-pricked Grisk, too. And tonight, Eben had gained the attentions of a handsome, burly Ash-Kai named Othan, who stroked him with cautious, clever hands, as his hard, hungry prick plumbed deep inside.

"Ach, sweet Ka-esh," Othan grunted, falling free of Eben's spasming body with a squelch, before plunging back inside, seating himself deep in a single unbroken stroke. "Can you always take it this easy and deep? Ach, I ken I have reached your"—he gasped, as Eben purposefully clutched him—"your *heart*."

It betrayed a shocking lack of anatomical awareness, or even basic education, but in this moment, Eben didn't care. Not with this much hard prick buried inside him, taking pleasure with him, pumping its seed deep. Not as deep as that Skai would have gone, no, and Othan's prick didn't boast a single scar, either. But Othan was fucking Eben, now, and Eben belatedly, fervently nodded, clamping tighter against that thick pulsing prick.

"You can go harder, too, if you like," he breathed over his shoulder, his usual hesitations blessedly buried beneath the pleasure and the frenzy, the stark desperate craving. "Use your claws and teeth, or a switch, or a whip. Whatever you please."

But behind him, Othan's chuckle was hoarse and disbelieving, his big hands carefully caressing Eben's shivering flanks. "Couldn't harm you, sweet Ka-esh," he gasped. "Wish for your joy, ach?"

Eben had to choke down the surge of dark, bitter frustration, but he appeased himself with driving back deeper onto Othan's prick, sinking into the sensation of it, the challenge of gripping it as hard as he could, locking it into place. And that was enough to make Othan wrench all over, crying out shocked and shrill—and yes, yes, there was his seed, flooding fast and abundant into Eben, filling his empty places from the bottom up, until he felt almost full, almost, *almost* content.

Afterwards, Othan wanted to kiss and cuddle him, but Eben suddenly couldn't bear his touch, the longing in his eyes—and his desperate glance around the room thankfully settled on Gareth, who'd just finished with the excessively beautiful Julian, his first fuck of the evening. And Gareth was a good friend, a generous Ka-esh clanmate, because upon seeing the look on Eben's face, he instantly came over toward them.

Not sparing a single glance for Othan as he smiled at Eben, and reached to slide a slow, suggestive hand against his arse.

"Ready for more, brother?" Gareth asked, and yes, he was already turning Eben around, guiding him away from Othan. "Wish for some steel in your rump, this time?"

Eben furiously nodded, and shot what he hoped was an apologetic smile toward Othan's rather crestfallen face. And when Gareth shoved Eben double, he gratefully arched and opened for Gareth's familiar prick, hissing with the sweet, stunning pain of it slamming inside.

The pain was due to Gareth's multiple solid steel piercings, which were embedded not only in his cleft, but all the way down his shaft. They'd sent more than one orc to the sickroom, Eben knew, but he usually had enough control to handle it, to make himself open when he needed to, and not to let that steel-studded head anywhere near the delicate tissues deeper within. But today, his control seemed frayed, lost somewhere else, and he choked aloud at the sudden scrape of pain, the distinct scent of blood as Gareth drew out again.

"All right, brother?" Gareth asked behind him, his voice sharp with genuine concern, and Eben had to draw in a shaky breath, squeezing his eyes shut. No. Foolish. He would not weep over being asked a stupid single question, and he knew Gareth didn't care, not like that. As thoughtful and considerate as Gareth usually was, Eben knew how deeply he longed for someone who would fight him over the pain, who would greet his grating invading steel with vengeance and teeth. But Eben was not that kind of orc, had never been that kind of orc, Eben wanted... he wanted...

"Ach, I am well," Eben belatedly replied, and then he twitched and gasped at the sweet, surprising sensation of Gareth's breath, his slick seeking tongue, delving into his open, dripping crease, licking at his fresh wound. A gift, truly, and

Eben fought to keep Othan's seed inside, away from Gareth's lovely licking mouth. "Th-thank you."

He could already feel the pain prickling, fading beneath the wondrous analgesic of orc saliva, and when Gareth stood tall behind him again, perhaps hesitating, Eben blatantly arched and opened himself, as wide as he could. Shuddering at the feel of Othan's hot seed escaping, streaking liberally down his trembling thighs, but he knew Gareth didn't care about other orcs' seed on his prick, and oh, he was already leaning forward and nudging in again, more gently this time.

"You are sure?" Gareth asked, pushing in with a little more certainty, until Eben stopped it, clamped him tightly in place. "Naught is amiss? I thought"—his voice dropped as he drew out again—"you should have welcomed an orc such as Othan ploughing you thus, and wishing to tend you and fuss over you, after."

Eben couldn't hide his wince, or his shameful, foolish reply, not with the beautiful strength of Gareth's steel dragging deep inside him. "Ach, I should have welcomed this," he gasped, squeezing his eyes shut. "But today, I was in the—Skai wing, and I—"

His voice failed him there, his thoughts blooming with the vision of the tall Skai's fat, scarred, dripping prick, his quick, approving smile. While behind him, Gareth's thrusts slowed, and Eben could feel his focus now, could taste the surprise in his scent. "You did not—mate with a Skai, did you?" he asked. "I cannot scent this upon you...?"

He left the question dangling, and Eben shook his head, shoved back a little harder onto that scraping steel. "No," he said, too insistent, too betraying. "But I—"

He... what? He could have done it? He'd wanted to do it? He'd wanted to wander aimlessly about the Skai wing, and then turn around, and find that tall, smiling orc again. And in another realm, one where Eben was calm and confident and desirable, he might have smiled and said, *It turns out I am lost after all, good sir. Would you show me the way?*

Foolish, his distant thoughts chanted, and he again shook his head, focused on staying soft for that sweet sliding steel. "It was foolish," he croaked. "There was just one who was—kind. Helped me. Not like—I thought."

He winced again, shaking his head, because a moment's kindness in a corridor had nothing to do with an entire clan's sins, with the path of Ka-esh grief and devastation the Skai had left in their wake for the past half-century. And it made no sense for Eben to even notice that Skai, or care, let alone to have him ruin a perfectly good evening of perfectly good ploughing pricks.

"You ken we cannot judge a whole clan upon the actions of some, many years past," came Gareth's slow, thoughtful voice behind Eben, in strong contrast to how his steel-studded prick was sinking in faster now, scattering out jolts of pain and pleasure around it. "You ken the Skai have new leaders now, and they are seeking these new ways, ach? And seeking to make amends for their past sins."

Eben nodded, shifting his upper body heavier against the wall, feeling the welcome scrape of rough stone against his sweaty skin. "But they still aren't even following the rules," he gasped, because it was the only safe statement he could grasp at, in the whirling mess now clouding his thoughts. "They were openly fucking in the corridor!"

His voice came out sounding inordinately irate, and he fully deserved Gareth's amused chuckle behind him, the sharper thrust of his hips. "I had you outside the forge just last week, did I not?" he said wryly. "What is the harm, if there are only orcs of age within scenting distance? We all know what is afoot, whether it is before our eyes, or no."

But there *was* a harm, Eben's aggravated thoughts pointed out. A harm of some clumsy, unsuspecting fool Ka-esh walking past, and not being able to look away. Not being able to stop thinking of that tall, stunning Skai, and his beautiful scarred prick. A prick that would be a true joy to milk and squeeze, to welcome deep inside, into one's most tender places...

And it would be a joy to drink from, too. For those scars, those teeth-marks, laddered up the Skai's prick, meant that he often offered the gift of his fresh blood and seed together—and there was no other taste like it in all the realm. Eben's own extensive research had suggested that there was no other nourishment like it, either, nothing else that would better fatten a sick or weakened or weary orc.

And even the thought of it, of that stunning smiling Skai offering it, was drawing up Eben's bollocks, coiling the longing tight and close. But he suddenly couldn't bear to empty himself on the vision of this, the too-powerful memory of this, and therefore welcome even more of that Skai's destruction, his devastation, without even a touch—

"Could you use—the switch," he gasped over his shoulder. "Or the whip. Please."

Gareth's breath huffed against Eben's sweaty back, but he accordingly reached up to the well-stocked wall beside them, and pulled down a short, coiled whip. But even as he unfurled it, giving an experimental little snap into the air, his other hand stroked at Eben's flank, perhaps felt the heavy dragging of his gasping breaths.

"There's naught wrong with broadening your view of others, as you grow older and wiser," Gareth's low voice said, even as the whip's fall gently teased at Eben's back. "And naught wrong with desiring a Skai, either."

Eben knew that, of course he knew that—broadening views along with desires was embedded deep in the Ka-esh clan's very soul, was it not? And he rapidly, fervently nodded, but the lash still didn't strike, just kept taunting and trailing like that, making him pay attention, making him listen.

"I ken you only need to learn more," Gareth continued, slower. "To mayhap watch them for a spell, and see what they do, and how they live. How they treat their kin and those they care for. What they long for, in their kin, and their mates. And then, after this"—a very gentle, teasing swat of the lash—"you can choose what to do with this. Whether you should welcome a Skai into your life, or your bed."

It was sound advice, Eben could admit, and far more generous than he likely deserved. And far more presumptuous, too, because Eben wasn't nearly interesting or compelling enough for any Skai to want in his bed, most of all a Skai like that—but even so, he couldn't help his swift, grateful smile over his shoulder, his eyes warm on Gareth's flushed face. Feeling how Gareth's cock had swelled larger, too, scraping his walls with that sweet sharp steel, while the whip raised high, quivering in the air...

And with a hiss and a splatter, Eben was breaking beneath the lash, the Skai finally, blissfully forgotten amidst the pain and the screams.

3

For the next few weeks, Eben followed Gareth's good guidance, and just... observed.

It was his natural state, borne of many years of shyness, self-consciousness, and solitary, scholarly pursuits. And though he only caught a few brief glimpses of the tall, smiling orc from the corridor, he instead focused his attention on the Skai orcs he did encounter, most of whom had ended up in the sickroom with various illnesses or injuries.

And the more Eben observed, the more he found himself... surprised. Many of the Skai bore harsh faces and curt, dismissive demeanours, which—together with all the tales and warnings—had always been enough to keep him at a safe, careful distance. But upon further inspection, even when a wounded Skai snapped sharply at the sickroom staff, or glowered viciously toward any other patients who came too close, he would frequently soften when offered any kind of unexpected generosity, or when loved ones came to visit. A huge, horribly injured orc named Ulfarr had nearly wept when his friend Killik had shown up with a basket of snacks, and Simon, the massive and terrifying Enforcer of Orc Mountain, had fully ignored his painful cracked femur in favour of doting upon his mate and son from his bed.

And when Eben had gathered his courage one afternoon, and collected some sweet treats from the kitchen to distribute to a handful of wounded Skai, they'd been surprised, and grateful, and even *kind*—at least, until one big, blood-covered warrior had blatantly looked Eben up and down, and invited him into his bed. An invitation that had instantly sent Eben fleeing back for the safety of his workbench, while Efterar had snapped a sharp reprimand across the room. And in return, the orc—much to Eben's surprise—had blushed, and winced, and *apologized*.

But the most enlightening situation of all happened perhaps a half-moon later, with the unexpected arrival of a new patient—a blonde, grievously injured human woman named Alma. Her pale, weakened body had been covered with contusions and lacerations, and she'd inhaled smoke and particulates at length, before almost drowning in a river. She had only survived thanks to a daring rescue by a prominent Grisk orc named Baldr, who served as the Left Hand to Orc Mountain's captain—but during the rescue, Alma and Baldr had formed a deep, irrevocable scent-bond. Which wasn't surprising, perhaps, given the high emotions and close physical proximity inherent in such an event—except for the fact that Baldr was already mated to the mountain's Right Hand, a tall, glowering Skai named Drafli.

Eben had always found Drafli highly alarming, for he seemed the epitome of the cold, vicious, dangerous Skai. He prowled instead of walked, he reeked of human blood and death, and he only spoke with sharp, furious gestures, due to having had his throat cut by humans, whom he had then gone and killed with his bare hands. Drafli was widely acclaimed as the best, most terrifying fighter in the mountain, and Eben had often heard hushed, awed whispers of his many exploits in the Skai arena—along with his many conquests in pleasure, none of whom he had ever appeared to notice, let alone favour.

But at some point the year before, Drafli had strongly endorsed that change to the Skai mating customs, and had immediately sworn vows to this Baldr. Drafli had been the first Skai in living history to take an orc mate... and now, not even a full year later, his new mate had turned about and formed a permanent, unbreakable scent-bond with a human woman.

It was a situation that would have been highly trying for any orc, especially a Skai as notorious as Drafli—but to Eben's genuine astonishment, Drafli hadn't shown even the slightest hint of anger toward his wayward mate. Each night, once most of the sickroom's inhabitants were asleep, Drafli and Baldr would come and sit beside the unconscious Alma's bed, and Drafli would firmly caress Baldr, and kiss his hair. And even across the room, Eben could easily trace their fresh strong scents upon one another, untainted by any others. Meaning that Drafli had continued to bed his mate, and favour him, despite the betrayal of the scent-bond with the woman.

"You should leave me, Draf," Eben heard Baldr whisper into Drafli's neck, on the third night of this. "Go find someone else. Someone stronger. Better."

There were no other orcs awake in the room to hear this—Efterar and his ever-present mate Kesst had gone out together on a call—and Eben held his breath as he listened, his body quiet and unmoving behind his workbench. Waiting, watching, as Drafli wordlessly hissed back at his mate, his clawed hands snapping out movements between them— speaking something in the Skai clan's sign language, something Baldr answered with a choked sob, and a shake of his head.

But Drafli said it again, and again—and when Baldr kept

weeping, Drafli whirled up, grasped him by the neck, and... *attacked*. Shoving Baldr down hard to the bed, so he could straddle over him, and... *kiss* him.

Oh. Ohhhh. Eben startled, his breath choking in his throat—but if they'd noticed him, neither of them seemed to care. Instead, Baldr's eyes had fluttered with palpable longing, his body pressing into the scrape of Drafli's claws, the deep, dragging bite of his kiss. And when Drafli drew away, and then shoved Baldr over onto his front, Baldr only moaned and arched for him, even when Drafli's clawed hand yanked down his trousers, exposing Baldr's muscled, trembling arse to the room.

For a breath, Drafli only gazed down at that bared arse with hooded eyes, his hand curving slow and proprietary over its smooth green skin—and then he shoved at his own trousers, too. Releasing his own long, bobbing, leaking prick, with vivid scars laddered all the way up its grey length.

Eben shivered all over, his vision briefly blurring, and suddenly it was as though he was back in the corridor, watching that tall, laughing Skai. Because Drafli's prick looked far too much the same, jutting hard and hungry from above sagging trousers, seeking its way between quivering arse-cheeks... and then slamming deep with a sharp slap of skin, while his helpless lover gasped and writhed beneath it.

Fuck. And though a distant part of Eben pointed out that this was certainly against the rules—what with all the sleeping patients in the room—he couldn't seem to move, let alone speak, caught in the vision before his eyes. Baldr flinching and writhing and moaning beneath his Skai mate's onslaught, the look on his face pulling low and familiar in Eben's belly, whispering of that perfect mingled pleasure and pain...

Drafli even kept speaking in their sign language as he drove inside, one hand swiftly moving before Baldr's fluttering eyes, while his mouth kissed and scraped at Baldr's shoulder. As his hips kept snapping him in deeper, faster, flooding all his mate's senses at once—and Eben nearly staggered beneath the scent of Baldr's lurching, shattering release, sweeping across the room, while Drafli's thrusts slowed into sweet, steady circles, his lips gently kissing at his trembling mate's neck.

It was a dazzling display of skill and force and tenderness, the kind of attention that would have had Eben blatantly spreading and begging in the *dýflissa*. And before he could compromise himself any further, he belatedly rushed for the sickroom's back latrine, yanked down his trousers, and took his own straining prick in hand. And as he stroked, the visions swarming his scattering thoughts were again all that tall, laughing Skai in the corridor, touching his own bent-over lover with that same heady blend of skill, tenderness, and command. Sliding his fat, scarred length in and out, again and again, while the orc moaned and shuddered beneath his sharp claws, that firm slap of his hand...

Eben gasped as his release sprayed out, shooting down the latrine in furious arcs of spurting seed and sweet, shattering pleasure. *You like that? More, sweet thing. I can show you the way...*

But once it was done, Eben's body felt shaky and weak, his heartbeat pounding far too loud against his ribs, his skull. And he sank heavily back to the nearest wall, gulping down deep breaths, and rubbing at his eyes.

Fuck, what had come over him? He was only meant to be observing, learning, not drowning in lust over a random Skai in the corridor. And not longing for what he'd just witnessed, either, aching all over at the thought of a deadly, capable mate who would offer such loyalty, such unflinching care and kindness, even amidst his own loss and pain...

It took far too long for Eben to collect himself, to walk on shaky legs back out toward the sickroom. Where he instantly caught sight of Baldr, now sprawled in the bed with his eyes closed, his scent speaking of quiet, steady sleep. While Drafli was... he was...

Drafli was standing tall and silent over the sleeping woman's bed, and holding a sharpened dagger over her throat.

4

Drafli was going to kill her.

Eben froze to shocked, horrified stillness, as alarm blared and screeched behind his eyes.

Never trust a Skai, never trust a Skai...

Drafli's head whipped around toward Eben with sudden, deadly purpose, his eyes snapped to narrow slits, his lip curled to show all his sharp teeth. As if he would kill Eben, too, without hesitation or regret—and Eben needed to run, to hide, to collapse the nearest tunnel behind him. Or maybe dash back into the latrine and cower in a corner, wait for the sweet scent of human blood to filter through the air...

But no. No. He couldn't. He *couldn't*. The woman was a patient, she was defenseless, she was Eben's responsibility. And that certainty was enough to make Eben draw in a shaky, shallow breath, to focus his hazy eyes on the vicious, murderous Skai with the dagger. The Skai who looked so, so different from how he'd looked only a short time ago, when he'd tended to his distraught mate with such intent, ardent care.

And that was something, something, and Eben drew in

more breath, desperately gathered his courage. "It will n-not—work," he croaked, into the empty, crackling silence. "To break the s-scent-bond. You will only—h-hurt your mate."

Drafli's flashing eyes darted back toward Baldr's sleeping body in the bed, and Eben clutched for the doorframe at his side, and hauled down another breath. "Y-you would not wish him b-bonded to a corpse in a crypt," he gulped. "And you would not wish him to—know, with every scent, that this was—your doing. This should—p-poison you, and him, and this—this deep trust you have, between you. This—gift."

He was fully trembling by the end of it, his claws clattering against the stone of the doorframe. And for an instant, staring at Drafli's coiled body, Eben was certain he would still do it. He would slit the woman's throat, and then hurl the dagger straight at Eben, too...

But then, Drafli—closed his eyes. Tilted his head back, as if in a brief, desperate prayer. And then he spun and stalked for the door, his shoulders rigid, his gleaming dagger still clasped tightly in his fist. And that might have been a faint, visceral shudder, quivering up his bare back, as he spun into the corridor, and vanished from sight.

Fuck. Eben didn't know how long he stood there, clinging to the wall, staring at the empty doorway, while his heart hammered sick and dizzying in his throat. *Never trust a Skai.*

He only vaguely noticed Efterar and Kesst finally returning to the sickroom, both their scents reeking of exhaustion. And though neither of them spared Eben a glance before falling into their own bed together, it was enough that Eben could somehow move again, could pry his numb fingers from the doorframe, and then stagger toward the door. Toward the Ka-esh wing. Toward—the *dýflissa.*

As always, it offered distraction and relief and pain, and as many dominant, powerful orcs as Eben could ask for. Some of them seeking his pleasure, some of them only his screams—

but no matter how much Eben begged for more, none of it was strong enough to fully clear the chaotic mess clouding his thoughts. And finally he dragged his sore, sweaty, bloody body back through the long corridors to his cold, empty bedroom.

Foolish, he told himself, as he lay there alone in his hard bunk, the pain pulsing through his torn back, his still-slack arse. *Foolish.* He'd done his job tonight, he'd helped protect his patient, and that was all. And in truth, he'd faced far worse throughout the course of his career as a medic, hadn't he? He'd witnessed horrifying grief and pain and regret, he'd wept as he'd heard dying orcs' last words, he'd saved and lost too many lives to count. So why did he even care so much about these damned Skai? Why was he still thinking about that laughing orc from the corridor, all these weeks later? Why was he still caught on this, trapped in this, when he had his own life, his own work, and as many willing Ka-esh lovers as he could ever ask for?

You never focus on what is important, Eben could still hear his father saying, with his typical frustration and disappointment leaching bitterly through his scent. *You waste your talent and your time. You do a deep disservice to all your Ka-esh kin. You show yourself foolish and weak.*

Eben sighed and shoved over in the bed, yanking the blanket off his sore back, but the ache was still there, scraping across his skin, wrenching deep in his belly. He'd tried, with his father. He'd tried so hard to please him, to study mathematics and geology, to become a master Ka-esh engineer. Just as his father had been, and his father before him.

But it had been such dull, dreary work, dragging at Eben's energy and his motivation. And his spare time spent with human anatomy books and medical research had been so much more intriguing, with so many more unexplored possibilities. There was just so much about orc biology that was yet fully unknown—from their inherent healing abilities, to the many properties of seed and saliva and blood, to the mysteries and devastating dangers of orc-human reproduction.

Eben's own mother had died during his birth, which he knew had happened in wartime, in highly unsanitary conditions deep underground. And thanks to his studies, he'd also learned that his own relatively small size was due at least in part to the fact that his mother would have seen little sun during her pregnancy, if at all—and she'd likely been lacking in the crucial nutrients humans needed from fruit, grains, and cooked meat.

And perhaps it was Eben's guilt and grief over his mother's death that had kept driving him back to those human textbooks again and again. Seeking out the answers that could help prevent such unnecessary deaths in the future, and maybe even help rebuild their species. And eventually Eben had progressed to making his own notes, too, keeping his own journals, and hiding it all from his increasingly enraged father.

You told them you wish to specialize in medicine, like a human? his father had demanded after a particularly trying day, during which a teenage Eben's distraction on a tunnel dig had led to the loss of three entire days' work. *You told them you wish to never dig a tunnel again?!*

Eben certainly hadn't meant to admit such things, let alone to fellow students who had become increasingly contemptuous toward him and his intelligence. But the grating endless tedium had been so strong, so utterly overwhelming, that he'd finally confessed it all to his father between gulping, gasping sobs. *I want to study medicine. I care about it, and I'm good at it. I want to learn, and help people. I want to help save our kin.*

His father had listened in stony silence, his scent hardening with every breath, and when Eben had finally finished, his father had raised himself tall, and pointed at the door. *Get out,* he'd said. *And do not return here or speak to me again, until you come to your senses.*

So Eben had left their familiar *hellir*, embedded deep with the scents of his ancestors, and with many scents of his own far happier childhood. And he'd gone as far away as he could, to the very edge of the Ka-esh wing, and found a small, dry room to sleep in. And he'd been here ever since, summer after summer, changing his path whenever he scented his father nearby, and averting his eyes whenever they met in a corridor. Until one morning he'd realized he hadn't scented his father in many days, and when he'd finally dared to return to the *hellir*, he'd found his father gravely ill and incoherent, scenting of whispering death.

So Eben had cared for his ill father with the full extent of his knowledge, easing the pain with the strongest herbs, bringing him fresh blood to drink, moving him regularly, even licking his bedsores to help him heal. And while it had without question made his father's final weeks more peaceful, it still hadn't saved his life—and Eben still didn't know if his father had even recognized him, let alone understood all that he'd done.

Eben was somehow weeping into his fur, the water streaking off his face in hot rivulets, the ache clutching again and again at his heaving chest. And here was the damned vision of the Skai again, smiling at him, so confident, so certain, so... pleased. So blithely, genuinely pleased by Eben's bringing his clanmate tonic, to the point where he'd offered his help. Maybe even his... pleasure.

Ach, I see. Good of you to bring it. Just come back if you get lost. I can show you the way.

It again heated in Eben's belly, so starkly, impossibly powerful, and tangling with it now were the clashing visions of Drafli, too. Cradling his lost mate so tenderly in his arms, drawing out his pleasure with such focused, single-minded purpose, as if he would never stop caring for him, would never hurt him or let him go...

And the way he'd stood over that sleeping woman, with pure hatred in his eyes, and his dagger flashing over her throat. Ready to kill a weakened, already-wounded patient, to snuff out her entire life, because she'd committed the unforgivable sin of being rescued by his mate, and succumbing to an orc-induced biological response she surely hadn't even known existed.

Never trust a Skai. Never let one touch you, or get you alone...

But Eben's sobs wouldn't stop coming, wracking through his aching body again and again and again. Until finally they drew him down with them, and locked him into lonely, empty sleep.

5

Eben slept badly that night, jolting awake again and again to visions of Drafli, of daggers, of death. Until he finally gave up and dragged himself out of bed, fighting to steady his thoughts and his breaths.

Perhaps last night had just been—a mistake, for Drafli. A moment of weakness. Perhaps he had learned his lesson, and would henceforth stay out of the sickroom, well away from the woman, where he could resist any murderous impulses he felt toward her. And perhaps if Baldr stayed away long enough, the scent-bond would eventually weaken, and this entire situation could be forgotten.

Eben's cautious optimism rose once he reached the sickroom, and found no sign or scent of Drafli or Baldr whatsoever. Alma's condition had also continued to improve overnight, to the point where Efterar had finally deemed her well enough to awaken—and she soon proved to be a shy, polite woman, who greeted the sickroom staff with quiet, earnest gratefulness.

"I—I'm truly sorry to have inconvenienced you, sir," she told Efterar, her voice thin and raspy through her still-compromised throat. "If you'd be so kind as to draw up the bill, I will—"

But Efterar firmly waved the matter away, as always, and began his usual patient briefing, while Eben pulled over Alma's chart and began adding notes. As usual, he and his fellow Ka-esh medic Salvi had been mixing daily tonics specifically tailored toward Efterar's ongoing assessments of her needs, and this would surely provide some helpful insights, and—

And then Baldr burst into the room, his eyes wide and panicked, his scent reeking of alarm. Suggesting, damn it, that the scent-bond was still exerting a considerable draw upon him, enough that he'd been able to sense Alma's awakening, from wherever he'd been. But wait, he'd likely been with *Drafli*—and yes, there, the scent faint but coming closer, was Drafli himself.

Eben's heart jolted in his chest, and his sweaty, shaky hand abruptly dropped his quill, smearing ink all over Alma's chart. Curse it, curse it—and though Eben frantically fought to mop it up, he didn't miss Alma's genuine-seeming pleasure upon seeing Baldr, or Baldr's ever-increasing scent of alarm as he also glanced toward the door. Toward where Drafli was now striding into the room, his head held high, his clawed hands hanging with dangerous casualness at his sides.

Eben only distantly noticed his own ink-stained hands clutching at the workbench, his heartbeat hammering louder in his ears. What would Drafli do now? Would he pull out a dagger, threaten Alma again, kill her before they'd even seen him move? Or, perhaps he would finally punish his mate for having succumbed to the call of the scent-bond, against whatever self-control he'd clearly found for the past day?

But in a jerky movement, Baldr spun and rushed straight toward Drafli, relief reeling through his scent. And rather than refusing, or pushing his mate away, Drafli instantly drew him closer. Sinking a possessive hand into Baldr's hair, guiding his head into his own shoulder, even as his eyes dangerously narrowed, glowering toward Alma in the bed.

Alma blanched, clutching her blanket to her chin, the scent of her fear sharpening in the air—and wait, wait, Drafli and Baldr were both moving *toward* her. Toward her, rather than away. And what the hell were they doing, was Baldr... making *introductions*?!

But no one in the room seemed to notice, or share Eben's rapidly rising panic. Efterar had already turned away to another patient, while beside Eben, Salvi was actually attempting to talk to him, speaking words Eben couldn't even slightly hear through the shrieking in his ears, and the scent of Drafli's ever-rising rage in his nostrils. A scent that was far too similar to the night before, to that moment when he'd held that dagger over Alma's throat—

Eben's body was already lurching, staggering over toward them, when suddenly Drafli spun around and stalked toward the door, his eyes blazing, his hands in fists. Leaving Baldr to trail unhappily after him, his scent reeking of misery and pain, while Alma had already curled up beneath her fur, and the sounds of her soft, sniffling sobs began scraping through the room.

"You all right, brother?" Salvi's distant voice cut in, as his elbow nudged into Eben's side. "Not feeling ill yourself, are you?"

Eben's breath exhaled in a harsh, shaky sigh, and he rapidly shook his head, and forced his focus back to his work. But it was a miserable way to spend a morning, breathing in the scents of a helpless human's anguish, while casting constant worried glances toward the door. And even when Alma fell asleep again, Eben could still scarcely concentrate, making multiple foolish errors mixing his tonics, until Salvi finally dragged him off for a meal with him and his Ka-esh mate

Tristan. And while Eben considered them both good friends, and made a concerted attempt to chat and smile through his misery, he returned to work feeling even more bleary and exhausted than before.

But at least there had been no further sign of Drafli or Baldr, and Alma was awake again, sitting up in her bed, and even weakly smiling at Efterar's mate Kesst, who was clearly plying her with all his considerable charm. But Alma's eyes were still puffy and swollen, her scent laced with misery and unease that echoed Eben's own—especially when Kesst shot a sly, assessing glance across the room toward the workbench. Toward—Eben?

"Have you met any of our orcs yet?" Kesst asked Alma, his voice deceptively light. "If you're feeling up to it, maybe one of them could give you a tour? How about you, Eben?"

What? Wait, was Kesst implying that Eben—*liked* Alma? Like that? Enough to personally take her on a damned *tour*, where a murderous Drafli might emerge at any moment?! And curse it, Eben's hands were suddenly spasming again, sloshing his jar of blood thinner all over the workbench—to which Kesst triumphantly smirked, while Alma flushed, scenting of both flattery and chagrin. And beside Eben, Salvi cursed under his breath as he snatched Eben's priceless notebook to safety, and then tossed a rag into his hot face.

Eben wiped up the mess as well as he could, though his cheeks wouldn't stop burning, and he couldn't even hear the rest of their conversation through the ringing in his ears. But finally, it seemed that Kesst had offered to take Alma on the mountain tour himself, and soon they were leaving the room together, Alma's steps still slow and halting, while Kesst cheerfully chattered away beside her.

Eben helplessly watched them go, his miserable alarm jolting higher—surely even Drafli wouldn't attempt to kill Alma in the corridor, with multiple witnesses?—until Salvi bumped him with his shoulder, his familiar scent tasting of both amusement and exasperation. "What the hell's going on with you today, brother?" he asked under his breath. "You aren't actually interested in her, are you?"

In Eben's exhausted state, he couldn't stop his incredulous glare back, because Salvi should know better by now, shouldn't he? "*Ach*, no," he replied, too sharp. "I am only... tired, I ken."

He reflexively shifted on his feet as he spoke, wincing at the distant pain still nagging in his sore back and arse—and Salvi instantly followed the movement, comprehension flaring across his eyes. "Ach, now I follow," he said cheerfully. "Took things too far in the *dýflissa* again last night, then? Mayhap you should have Efterar take a look at it?"

He'd angled a meaningful glance across the room toward Efterar, who was blearily working over a sleeping Bautul patient, but Eben grimaced, shaking his head. "Ach, no," he said again. "It was foolish. I shall heal."

Salvi's sidelong glance was a little too knowing this time, but he shrugged, and dipped his quill in the ink. "I heard Othan was asking about you yesterday," he said, as he began writing in his notebook. "He's a decent fellow, ach? Would treat you like you're made of gold."

Eben grimaced again, frowning down at his own notebook, as yet more misery plunged in his belly. Because that wasn't at all what he wanted, was it? He didn't want some bigger, stronger orc doting upon him, condescending to him, as if Eben was some kind of weak, fragile, stupid little pet... right? Or did he, and the memories of the laughing Skai orc were surging again, with his cool commands, his dragging, petting claws. *I can show you the way...*

And curse it, what the hell was wrong with Eben? Why was he still so caught on this? He'd surely observed more than enough Skai behaviour by now, to the point where he'd nearly witnessed a Skai murdering an innocent victim. He needed to pull himself together, and distance himself from this entire situation, and...

And just then, Alma rushed back into the room. Her head ducked low, her hands over her mouth, the bitter scents of her terror and pain swarming sudden and sickening through the air. And Eben couldn't move, couldn't think, as he watched her stagger toward her bed on shaky legs, before hurling her weakened body beneath her fur, and bursting into sobs.

"That vile prick Drafli," Kesst snarled from where he'd stalked in behind her, his eyes flashing on Efterar's confused face. "He was openly fucking Baldr in the baths, when he *knew* we were going that way! And then Drafli *lost* it on her, flailing and growling and spitting at her, while Alma begged and wept and *apologized* to him! Promised him she'd leave the mountain forever, so he'd never have to look at her again!"

Damn it. *Damn* it. Eben's stomach twisted and plunged, the bile roiling in his throat—so it hadn't been murder, but perhaps it very nearly had been. Perhaps it soon still would be. And what was he supposed to do, he should have told someone, he should have found help, confessed it all to someone stronger and wiser, who would know how to keep her safe. *Never trust a Skai, never, never, never...*

It was too close, too certain, too strong to bear, and Eben croaked an incoherent excuse to Salvi, and then rushed for the door. Not looking as he dodged into the corridor, his head ducked low, his breaths gasping and shallow, so thin he didn't even scent the orc striding around the corner—

Until he crashed straght into him.

The impact sent Eben reeling backwards, almost colliding with the wall behind him, as shock and humiliation flooded through his chest. And he couldn't even make his prickling eyes focus on the orc, the orc whose strong hands were grasping his shoulders, holding him still...

"Ach, Ka-esh!" the orc exclaimed, in a smooth, alarmingly familiar voice. "Watch where you're headed, ach?"

No. No, no, no. But Eben's blinking, burning eyes were squinting hard now, fighting to see in the too-bright light of the nearby lamp. And finding a handsome, horribly familiar face...

It was him. The laughing orc from the corridor. The Skai.

6

The Skai was here. Outside the sickroom. Looking at Eben. *Touching* Eben. And...

Ach, Ka-esh! Watch where you're headed.

And... chastising him. *Correcting* him.

The bitter, miserable humiliation swelled higher in Eben's chest, and he belatedly shook his head, squeezed his eyes shut. "I am—sorry," he gulped, without looking at the orc's face. "I only did not—"

But his voice broke there, because what? He hadn't looked? He hadn't scented? He was an orc, he was Ka-esh, he knew how to navigate without vision, had all his life, so why was he—why was he—

Why was he almost weeping, here in the damned corridor. What was wrong with him, what was happening to him, maybe he should march himself straight back to Efterar and—

"I am—sorry, sir," he gasped, pleading, blinking back up toward the orc's face. "It shall not—happen again."

He jerked backwards, twisting away, toward the distant safety of the Ka-esh wing—but nothing happened. Nothing moved. Because the orc's hands were still holding him here, his grip strong and firm against Eben's trembling shoulders.

"Ach, no need to apologize, Ka-esh!" the orc replied, a little rushed. "An' no need to scent thus, either! Didn't mean to vex you."

His voice had softened as he'd spoken, and Eben blinked blearily up at his handsome, too-close face, at the strange look in his eyes. At something almost like—concern?

"It is—quite all r-right," Eben stammered, his voice not even slightly his own. "I was—careless. Foolish."

The orc's brow creased, and one of his hands gave Eben's shoulder a little squeeze. "Ach, don't speak thus, Ka-esh," he said firmly. "No harm done, you ken?"

He squeezed Eben's shoulder again, his gaze searching but genial on Eben's face. On where Eben was blatantly staring back, curse it, and he swallowed hard, and attempted a nod. "Th-thank you," he croaked. "That is—very kind."

The orc flashed him a stunning, relieved smile, and gave a dismissive wave of his graceful, long-fingered hand. "No need to thank me, Ka-esh," he said. "Happy to help."

With that, he released Eben's arms, gave him a jaunty little wink, and then spun and strode toward... the sickroom. The sickroom? As if—he hadn't scented of illness, had he?

Eben wasn't moving, wasn't breathing, was now just straining to listen as the orc's voice carried out the sickroom door. "Just wanted to see how the new woman's faring," he was saying. "Can I bring her anything? Treats? A clean fur, mayhap?"

Eben blinked, because surely this orc had no association whatsoever with Alma... did he? Or perhaps—perhaps *he* was attempting to court her? Perhaps he carried that seemingly ubiquitous longing for women borne by so many of their kin?

Something cold had begun scraping up Eben's spine, and

he was distantly gratified to hear Kesst's loud, derisive scoff. "What, have *you* developed a secret passion for Alma too, Tryggr?" he demanded. "Rest assured, she does not need any more Skai involvement in her life right now!"

Eben's body jolted all over, his heart skipping a beat in his chest. The orc's name was Tryggr. *Tryggr*. And Eben wanted to bless Kesst, curse Kesst, and what would this Tryggr say to being greeted like this, having his clan brought into this...

"Never spoken to the woman in my life," came Tryggr's voice, just a shade cooler than before. "An' haven't the slightest interest in her, either. But she's Boss's responsibility now, and since I'm working with Boss these days, I'm here to do my part."

Oh. Comprehension flared across Eben's thoughts, staggering him heavily against the nearby wall. This Tryggr worked with *Drafli*. And yes, Drafli did command his own small team of Skai scouts and fighters, didn't he? But... why would he send one of them to check on Alma? To help her? Because she was *Drafli's responsibility*?

Kesst seemed to share Eben's confusion, and another loud scoff filtered out through the doorway. "How is Alma Drafli's responsibility in any way whatsoever?" he demanded. "If you haven't heard, *he's* the one who just raged at her in the baths, and sent her running back here weeping!"

There was an instant's hanging silence, during which Eben fervently wished he could see this Tryggr's face—but when Tryggr spoke again, his voice was still smooth, almost deceptively easy. "Ach, I have heard of this, and wished to offer any help. But I'm glad you've got her looked after, and you'll keep a close eye on her, ach? Make sure she don't do anything rash?"

Kesst scoffed again, sounding highly affronted this time. "You can assure Drafli we have the situation well in hand," he drawled back. "And as if Alma's going to do anything rash in this state! Because of *him*!"

Another instant's stillness rang through the air, followed by a familiar low murmur—Efterar, no doubt seeking to settle his fractious mate. But there was no reply from this Tryggr, and suddenly he was—here. *Here*, striding out the sickroom door again, his head held high, his hands in fists—and no, Eben couldn't move in time, and Tryggr's shoulder knocked painfully into him, sending him reeling back against the wall.

Damn it, *damn* it, because Tryggr had already whirled around toward Eben, his eyes blazing. And Eben flinched, cringing backwards, bracing himself for this Tryggr's anger, or—or worse, his mockery. His inevitable realization that Eben had been shamefully lurking, eavesdropping on that entire conversation, and—

And then Tryggr's eyes... stilled. Softened. And that was a wry laugh, a shake of his head, as his hand came to Eben's shoulder, gave it a gentle squeeze.

"Sorry, Ka-esh," he said, hoarse. "Now I'm the one not seeing where I'm going! Some Skai I am, to not be able to walk down a hall without crashing."

He laughed again, but there was still a twinge of darkness in his eyes. And somehow Eben's commiseration was drowning out the alarm and shame, a wavering smile twitching at his mouth.

"N-no harm done," he managed, echoing Tryggr's own words from before. "Naught to apologize over."

The recognition shimmered across this Tryggr's eyes, and his smile flashed higher, warmer. "Ach, just so, Ka-esh," he replied. "Was just a bit worked up, I ken. That Ash-Kai is a real rabble-rouser, ain't he? No wonder you were in the same state last time we crashed. Must need a shocking amount of breaks, round here."

Oh. Eben couldn't help his own shaky laugh, or his deep, sudden surge of gratefulness toward this Tryggr. Because not only had Tryggr not judged him for lurking and eavesdropping in the corridor—but now he was identifying with him, and *sympathizing* with him, over *Kesst*. And while Eben personally found Kesst highly trying, he was also a very handsome, popular, charismatic orc, who was mated to the mountain's brilliant, universally respected Chief Healer—and thus, Eben had never heard anyone speak such blasphemy about him, not once. Or rather, not until now, until this Tryggr, and it felt warm and tenuous in his chest, almost about to burst. And Eben couldn't stop looking at Tryggr, smiling at Tryggr, even as his mouth opened on its own, about to say...

"But—why would Drafli send you to check on Alma?" his cursed voice asked, before he could stop it. "Or consider her—*his* responsibility? I thought..."

I thought Drafli wanted to kill her, he very nearly said, but he belatedly winced and clamped his fool mouth shut, and shook his head. What the hell was he saying, how had he become this much of a mess, he should still turn around and run, and...

"Ach, well, the woman's bonded to Boss's mate, ain't she?" Tryggr replied, and when Eben blinked at him, he was casually shrugging, his eyes easy and genial, as if there'd been nothing unusual whatsoever about Eben's question. "I ken it hasn't been an easy tangle to deal with, but Boss still won't want to see her come to harm. Wouldn't want to risk hurting his mate, you ken."

He spoke with such blithe confidence, without even a trace of guile in his voice—and Eben couldn't help frowning at him, the skepticism studding too strong in his own scent. "But how can you... be sure?" he asked thickly. "How can you know Drafli might not rather just... be rid of her?"

Tryggr blinked, but then shook his head. "He wouldn't," he said firmly. "Boss swore vows to his mate, swore to protect him with his life, and Skai don't take vows lightly, ach? An' besides"—he darted an irritable glance toward the sickroom door—"he specially asked me to come check in on her just now, ach? No doubt knew he'd be run off by that snippy Ash-Kai if he came himself—not that I fared much better, I ken."

He huffed a wry, regretful laugh, and gave another companionable squeeze to Eben's shoulder. Because wait, he was still touching Eben, had been touching Eben throughout all this—and perhaps it was that touch, that steady certainty, that seemed to inexplicably settle Eben's stiff shoulders, his breath slowly exhaling. And somehow, the tight knot of dread and misery that had been festering in his chest all these past days had finally seemed to... loosen, sinking into a strange, shaky relief. As if he almost... *believed* this orc. This *Skai*.

"Naught to fret over, Ka-esh," Tryggr said now, with a reassuring little shake to his shoulder. "Boss won't harm her. I ken he might not like her, or be glad she's here, and he's bound to lose his temper over it now and again. But he'll still want to make sure she's safe and looked after, so she can't bring any harm down on his mate. And if it makes you feel any better, we're all keeping an eye on him, too. Ach?"

The calm, confident certainty was still there, ringing in Tryggr's eyes and his voice and his scent, and for an instant, Eben's memory snapped backwards, to that moment with Drafli and the dagger. To how Drafli could have so easily have killed Alma, and Eben too—but he hadn't. He'd reconsidered it, and left. And despite his lapses in temper afterwards, he still hadn't made another actual murder attempt, had he? And did he really want Alma safe and looked after, could that be true, and maybe...

"Maybe I could—help you keep an eye on her," Eben blurted out, without at all meaning to. "On—on Alma, I mean. Let you know if aught is amiss."

Wait, was he saying that because he still didn't trust Drafli, or—curse him—because of this Tryggr. And Tryggr was blinking at him, something shifting in his eyes and his scent, something Eben couldn't at all read...

But then Tryggr jerked a curt nod, and his hand on Eben's shoulder gave him another firm little shake. "Y'know, that'd be good of you, Ka-esh," he said. "Real good. Thanks."

Real good. The praise flared and rippled up Eben's spine, pulled a small, shaky smile to his mouth. "Happy to help," he murmured, again echoing Tryggr's own words from before— and yes, yes, that was appreciation in Tryggr's eyes, in the new dimple quivering in his cheek. And oh, in the way he leaned in a little, his breath slowly inhaling, as if drawing in Eben's scent, lingering in it...

And fuck, Eben could scent him, too. Deep, and sweet, and rich. Strong enough that it watered in his mouth, stirred low in his groin...

"Then come to me whenever you need," Tryggr said now, leaning backwards again, giving Eben another quick smile, another bracing little shake. "I'll keep a nose out for your scent, ach?"

Right. *Right.* Tryggr had only been teaching himself Eben's scent, like any competent orc with a plan would do, and that was all. That was all, but it was still fizzling in Eben's belly, warming his eyes and his smile. He had a plan, with this Skai. With this... Tryggr.

And Tryggr was nodding again, and giving Eben one last companionable little shake before releasing his arm and striding down the corridor, away. His steps smooth and rolling, his soft black boots utterly silent on the stone floor, the dagger in his hair briefly gleaming in the lamplight. And Eben couldn't stop staring, drinking up the sight of him, of that lean strong back, that firm muscled arse in his trousers...

Never trust a Skai, his father's distant voice was droning, dragging up visions of Drafli with the dagger—but now another voice was rising, too. *No harm done. That'd be good of you, real good. Come to me whenever you need. I can show you the way...*

It seemed to keep shifting something, changing something deep and fundamental in Eben's thoughts. And he drew in a deep breath as he gazed down the empty corridor, tasted the remnants of Tryggr's sweet scent in the air.

Maybe he'd done enough observing. Maybe it was time... to act.

7

As he'd promised, Eben kept a close eye on Alma for the rest of the day, and well into the evening.

She'd mostly stayed huddled under her fur, either resting or sleeping, and she'd only stirred when spoken to, usually by Efterar, who had continued working over her throat. But she'd remained alive and unharmed, and Eben's breaths still came easier than before, his hands quick and efficient as he mixed tonics and medications for their patients.

He had a plan, with a Skai. With *Tryggr*.

He could almost still feel Tryggr's firm hands on his shoulders, could almost taste that sweet scent in the air—and he twitched all over when Tryggr himself strode back into the sickroom, early in the evening. His easy gaze catching on Eben at the workbench, and then darting down brief and curious to the tonic Eben was currently mixing. And though Eben's hands instantly began trembling, Tryggr didn't seem to notice, and he even gave Eben a quick, conspiratorial wink before striding across the room toward Efterar.

"How's the woman faring now, then?" Tryggr asked Efterar,

who was still hovering his hand over Alma's sleeping body. "Any better?"

Efterar gave a distracted, noncommittal shrug, while across the room, Kesst loudly scoffed. "Here again, Tryggr?" he demanded. "What, did you think we needed a helpful reminder of how Alma wouldn't even *be* in this state, if not for *your* so-called *Boss*?!"

Eben could see Tryggr stiffening, his hands clenching at his sides—but instead of retaliating in kind, he jerked a shrug, and strode back toward the door. His gaze briefly meeting Eben's on the way by, his expression shifting into something both aggrieved and amused as he gave an exaggerated roll of his eyes.

It sent even more warmth shivering up Eben's spine, and he willingly worked late into the night, only heading for bed once Efterar had firmly reassured him that he'd be staying with Alma until morning. And when Eben returned early the next day, Alma was indeed still sleeping safely in her bed, her scent noticeably brighter and clearer than it had been the night before.

"How's she doing now, then?" asked a cheerfully smiling Tryggr, when he strode back into the sickroom. "Scents better, don't she?"

Thankfully, Kesst was still asleep in a nearby bed, so Efterar was able to brief Tryggr without interruption. And when Tryggr left this time, he again winked at Eben, and—Eben startled—tossed him a shiny red apple before striding toward the door.

Eben scarcely managed to catch the apple, his face furiously burning, a foolish little smile pulling at his mouth. While beside him, Salvi—who Eben had nearly forgotten about—had abandoned his writing in favour of whirling around to stare at Eben, his scent surging with eager, gleeful curiosity.

"Who's the Skai?" he demanded. "And why's he bringing you *food*?"

Eben's mouth uselessly opened and closed, betraying far too much, damn it. And the gleefulness in Salvi's scent lurched even higher as his too-knowing gaze darted between Eben's hot face, the apple in his shaky hand, and the cursed obvious twitching in his trousers.

"Ach, it is naught," Eben began, too quickly. "He is only..."

But he couldn't finish, his face burning even hotter, because what *was* Tryggr, exactly? An acquaintance? A co-conspirator? The gorgeous, oblivious object of Eben's foolish, hopeless lust?

"Only your next bedmate, I ken," Salvi said, with a meaningful waggle of his eyebrows. "I ken you'll be reeking of Skai by the time we're back, ach?"

Salvi had been planning a fortnight-long trip north with Tristan, Eben knew, visiting a library Tristan had long wanted to see—and for the first time since he'd heard of it, Eben didn't feel even the slightest twinge of envy. "Ach, no," he said thickly, shaking his head. "I am sure—Tryggr would not. And I..."

His voice hitched, broke, and beside him Salvi laughed, and companionably bumped him with his shoulder. "Ach, I can scent you, brother," he said lightly. "You'll see."

Eben waved it away, but it still fluttered and shimmered in his chest, warm and eager and almost... hopeful. And it made it even easier to keep working, keep watching over Alma, feeling genuine relief at her steady, continued improvement. He had a plan. He could try to trust a Skai...

But then, around noon, Alma received an unexpected visitor. It was Lady Jule, who was mated to the mountain's captain—and though Jule was smiling and bouncing her orcling son in her arms, she had a distinct scent of grim purpose about her, as if she had unpleasant news to share.

Eben's rising suspicions soon proved correct, because after a few moments' pleasant chatting with Kesst and a bleary-looking Alma, Jule regretfully gave Alma her news. Apparently, Alma's dreadful former employer now regretted running her off, and had begun publicly claiming she'd been kidnapped by orcs—in strong violation of the tenuous peace-treaty between orcs and men.

Alma's already-pale face went white as she listened, her scent jolting with alarm and dread—but then she pulled herself straight in her bed, and gave a resigned little nod. "Well, I've been meaning to head back anyway," she said, her voice impressively steady, despite the sheer terror now ringing through her scent. "And I'm feeling much better, so I can certainly leave at once."

Eben's alarm had begun simmering too, not only because of Alma's highly distressed state, but because her leaving the mountain was exactly what Tryggr—and perhaps Drafli— would want to prevent. Wasn't it?

But wait, Kesst was already barking a loud, disapproving scoff, and jabbing his sharp claw toward Alma's cringing body in the bed. "You aren't going *anywhere*, sweetheart," he snapped. "Not until you're well again, and especially not back to that scum, who's likely to take out all his thwarted pettiness on you. It is *not* safe for you there. Eft, please come tell her she can't leave?!"

Efterar—who had just returned from a room call— promptly strode over and reinforced Kesst's position, even as Eben could see his focus on Alma's throat. On where she clearly wasn't yet fully healed, despite how she was sitting up straight, and arguing her point with surprising intensity. "But—I still need to go," she protested, blinking between Kesst and Jule with pleading eyes. "I told Baldr and Drafli I would leave, at once. It would be best, for everyone, if I go. I *promised* them, and Drafli said—"

She'd stopped there, perhaps due to the sudden fearsome glowering from Kesst and Jule, both of whom then launched into another bout of passionate arguments. Including the surprising revelation that Alma had apparently committed to helping out with the mountain's housekeeping, particularly in the scullery.

"Have you seen that hole, Jules?" Kesst demanded, his voice half-teasing, half-irate. "It is vile. *Vile!*"

Again, Eben found himself in reluctant agreement with Kesst—the mountain's former Keeper had recently retired, and in his absence, the mountain's lone scullery had been sorely neglected, and was now in an appalling state of disarray. To the point where most Ka-esh had quietly taken on the tedious but necessary task of doing their own laundry, deep in the underground cisterns.

But Alma's scent had slightly brightened at the mention of the scullery, so Kesst and Jule kept on, even more enthusiastic than before. "And maybe we can bring over some orcs to keep you entertained," Kesst's cheerful voice said, in the tone of one making a convincing closing argument. "And you can see if any of *them* tickle your fancy?"

Alma didn't appear at all enthused by this proposal, and beside Kesst, Jule huffed a laugh, and rolled her eyes. "*Kesst,*" she said. "Alma's not here to pick out an orc, like a new *pet.*"

But at that, Kesst's gaze darted over his shoulder, across the room, toward—toward *Eben.* "Are you sure?" he said lightly. "I don't think Eben would mind being Alma's new pet, right, Eben? *Especially* if there was a collar and lead involved?"

Wait. What? *No.* The sudden, startling mortification jolted through Eben's entire body—Kesst truly hadn't just said that, out loud, to a human *patient*?!—and Eben's shaking hand somehow lost its grip on the empty flask he'd been holding, which fell to the workbench with a hard, ringing *thunk.* Ensuring that every awake eye in the room was now trained curiously upon him, witnessing his red face and trembling hands.

And though he instantly dropped his eyes, and fought to drag in deep breaths, he could still feel all those eyes judging him, chastising him, mocking him. Fully believing Kesst's preposterous claim that he wanted to be a human woman's *pet*, on a collar and lead. Even when the human woman was already thoroughly involved with two orcs, one of them a terrifying Skai who Eben had prevented from *killing* her.

Eben barely heard the rest of their conversation over the ringing in his ears, and the waves of hot and cold shuddering up and down his spine. And though he forced himself to keep working—he'd promised Tryggr he would keep an eye on Alma, he'd *promised*—it was slow and stumbling, with far too many thoughtless errors. And all the hopeful shimmering warmth from earlier had vanished too, sinking back into the dark, bitter misery.

Foolish. Weak. You never focus on what is important...

And in truth, what had Eben been thinking, to begin imagining that he and Tryggr were co-conspirators, somehow? After they'd met only one day before, and shared a single conversation in the corridor? And of course a capable, confident Skai like Tryggr wouldn't be interested in a weak, foolish orc like Eben, who his colleagues mocked and belittled as little better than a pet.

To make matters worse, Tryggr didn't return for the rest of the day, and Alma also seemed to become increasingly morose, reeking of grief and anguish as she slipped in and out of sleep beneath her blanket. Until Eben could scarcely breathe through the scent of it, let alone focus on his work—a state that again wasn't helped by Kesst, who had now begun irritably pacing back and forth across the sickroom, and casting pointed glances toward Eben and Salvi at the workbench.

"You know," Kesst announced, to no one in particular, "I'm sure Alma would be so much happier if she had some help cleaning up that vile scullery. If some helpful Ka-esh would arrange to fix its clogged drain, maybe."

Eben attempted to ignore it and keep working, emulating Salvi's blithe obliviousness beside him, but Kesst just kept pacing, casting narrow glances toward him, again and again. Until finally Eben huffed a harsh, frustrated sigh, snapped his book shut, and rushed over to the stinking, filthy scullery. Where he dealt with the foul clogged drain himself, mucking it out until his arms ached, and his thoughts screeched with panic and misery. He was supposed to be keeping an eye on Alma, what if Tryggr returned, what if he'd missed him...

He was nearly frantic by the time he'd washed up and raced back to the sickroom, but—he jolted to a halt in the doorway—Alma still was huddled sleeping in her bed, and there was no fresh scent of Tryggr anywhere. And from the workbench, Salvi was frowning at Eben, with a stubborn glint in his eyes—and before Eben could take another step, Salvi strode over, grasped his shoulders, and steered him back out the door.

"Good night," Salvi called behind them. "See you tomorrow!"

It took Eben's exhausted brain far too long to realize what was happening—they weren't *leaving*?—and he wrenched to a halt in the corridor, rubbing at his aching eyes. "I can't leave again!" he croaked at Salvi. "Not yet. I need to make sure—I promised—"

But Salvi only gripped Eben's shoulders tighter, letting his claws dig in as he steered him back down the corridor. "You've been in there all damned day, brother," he snapped. "And all day yesterday too. Your scent smells awful, ach? You need rest."

Eben again attempted to argue, but Salvi fully ignored him, and kept marching him toward the Ka-esh wing. "Also, you shouldn't let Kesst get to you like that," he said, quieter. "The scullery's not your job, and that pet comment was just a stupid joke. Not worth your time, ach?"

But Eben's misery lurched even darker at the reminder of Kesst's joke, because why had the joke needed to be about him? Why had it needed to strike at his softest, weakest places, before a laughing audience? Because no, Eben didn't want to be a human's pet in the slightest, but maybe—maybe it had hurt so much because part of him *did* want something like it. Maybe part of him wanted a confident, capable companion to show up, and take him firmly in hand, and say, *No harm done. No need to apologize. Come to me whenever you need...*

Eben didn't argue again, just kept his head down as Salvi steered him through the corridors, and finally into his chilly, lonely room, deep in the Ka-esh wing. "Sleep," Salvi said. "And I'll see you in a fortnight, ach?"

Right. Eben couldn't deny another dark flare of misery— what would it be like, to have a mate who cared enough to take you to visit a *library*—but he managed a nod, and some semblance of a farewell. And though it was a vague relief to finally collapse into his bed, the misery just kept marching, circling through his weary brain. And tangling together with a distant, rising unease, something he couldn't quite name.

It would be—best, for everyone, if I go. I told Baldr and Drafli I would leave, I promised them, and Drafli said—

Eben could almost still taste the panic in Alma's voice as she'd said it, just the same kind of panic he would have felt in her place. Alma had seemed a thoughtful, considerate human, who wanted to pay her debts, and stay well out of trouble... and what would Eben do, if he was in her place? If he'd acquired not only the wrath of Drafli, but of an enraged former employer, too?

Eben shoved up in bed, staring at nothing in the darkness, as his heartbeat thudded in his chest—and then he scrambled up, yanked on his clothes, and staggered toward the door. He just needed to check. Just needed to be sure. He'd promised Tryggr, he'd sworn to take action on this, to try to trust a Skai...

Eben rushed up through the corridors without looking, his eyes shut tight against the too-bright light of the lamps as his breaths dragged in, and his heartbeat thundered louder and louder through his ears. It was probably nothing. It had to be nothing. He'd get to the sickroom and find Efterar still working, and Alma still curled up under her fur...

But the instant Eben reached the corridor, he knew something was wrong. Something was off in the scent. The scent of Alma here, in the corridor, where it wasn't at all supposed to be, and...

And even as Eben skidded into the sickroom, searching it with frantic eyes, the certainty was already there, blaring through his pounding skull.

Alma was gone.

8

For a jolting, jangling instant, Eben stared at the sickroom, at the handful of silent, sleeping orcs inside it. No Efterar. No Kesst.

No Alma.

Maybe Kesst and Efterar had taken Alma somewhere, maybe they'd gone off together—but no, no, Eben could follow Kesst and Efterar's scents leading that way, up the mountain, toward the Skai wing. While Alma's scent went... down. Out. Away...

She'd gone. Just as she'd promised to do.

Eben spun around, and ran. Sprinting with all his strength toward the Skai wing, his eyes searching in the blessedly dim light. His breaths dragging in harsh and deep, desperately seeking that sweet, familiar scent. Seeking Tryggr.

And yes, yes, that was Tryggr's scent, shimmering amidst the others, leading into the Skai wing—and Eben sprinted faster, skidding around corners, chasing the scent to its source. Deeper and deeper into the Skai wing, into an area he'd never before dared to visit, the light fading further with every step, while a distinct, unnerving noise grew louder, and louder. The noise of orcs, multiple orcs, shouting and grunting and screeching, with victory, and—and with pain. With... *pleasure.*

Eben slid to a stop before the source of the noise, blinking blankly through the open doorway, toward the sight before him. Toward the... room. And in the room was a mass of—chaos. Utter rioting chaos, teeming with shouts and bodies and hot, sweaty, bloody scents, clashing in a frenzied, clamouring mess into Eben's lungs.

They were... fighting?

But yes, they were fighting, and—a distant part of Eben's whirling brain pointed out—this had to be the Skai arena. He'd only never imagined it like this, with so many orcs packed in at once, not only scenting of Skai, but also dozens of Bautul, and a few Ash-Kai, too. And wait, over there, a grim-looking Efterar was crouched over a copiously bleeding Bautul, while Kesst stood beside him with arms crossed, his lip curled with palpable contempt.

There was no sign of Alma, of course—she was probably well beyond the mountain by now—and Eben's frantically searching eyes couldn't seem to find Tryggr, either. But Tryggr's scent had led here, to this, and he had to be here, Eben had to find him, he'd promised, he'd *promised*—

So Eben edged into the room, his heart furiously thundering as he kept close to the wall, his eyes darting all around, his breaths still swarming with the mass of overwhelming scents. Pain, and triumph, and frustration, and—yes, pleasure, because that Skai had pinned another Skai down by the hair, and was grinding against his bare, sweaty arse. And that Skai there was being taken by a big burly Bautul, moaning as his hips slammed deep—and that Skai had another Bautul kneeling before him, his hand clamped around the Bautul's neck, his scarred Skai prick gouging down his throat.

Eben watched for an instant too long, his groin shamefully stirring—and he forced his eyes shut as he crept further against the wall, dragging in deep, searching breaths. Tryggr was here, he had to be here, and maybe that, that, over there…

Yes, yes, that scented familiar, scented right, and Eben kept his eyes closed as he edged closer, and closer. Keeping his body pressed flat against the stone wall, he was almost, almost there—

"Ach, pretty Ka-esh," interrupted a voice, and Eben's eyes snapped open, his heart surging into his throat. Because no, no, there was a strange Skai, *here*, huge and sweaty and dripping fresh blood—and he was leaning in far too close, his breaths heavy and sour in Eben's nostrils.

"What brings a sweet small Ka-esh like you to the Skai arena, this night?" the orc crooned, his eyes alight on Eben's face. "Seeking some pleasure, I ken?"

Eben's heart wheeled up harder, his stomach twisting in his gut, and he clutched his claws at the wall, and wildly shook his head. "N-no, naught of the sort," he croaked. "I am only here for a moment. Only—seeking someone."

But the orc only leaned closer, and his huge clawed hand settled to the wall beside Eben's head, blocking him from moving forward. "Ach, are you?" he drawled. "Seeking someone who can make you kneel and beg, mayhap? Just as a good little Ka-esh should?"

What? Eben stared at the orc for an instant too long, as the heat and the misery pounded through his cheeks, against his screaming skull. No. No. This could not be happening. He should have known better, he should never have come here—

"No," he gasped, pressing himself back further against the wall. "No. Please. I am only here for—for—Tryggr."

His voice was badly wavering, enough that Tryggr's name was scarcely audible—but wait, the orc's beady eyes had darted sideways. Sideways, perhaps only a dozen paces away, where—yes—there was Tryggr, on the floor amidst the mass of fighting orcs. And he was grappling with another lean, handsome Skai, both of them laughing and gasping and snapping their teeth—but Tryggr clearly had the upper hand, straddling the other orc like that, pinning his wrists to the floor...

And then—Eben's heart lurched—Tryggr roughly shoved the other Skai onto his belly, and yanked down the orc's trousers. Revealing a hard, muscled grey arse, oh—and Tryggr's clawed hand gave it a swift, ringing slap before yanking down his own trousers, releasing his own swollen, scarred, dripping prick. The same prick that had filled so many of Eben's thoughts these past weeks—and it was now sliding easy and hungry between the orc's bared, quivering arse-cheeks. Seeking its place, finding it, and then sinking inside slow and deep...

No. No. *No.* Eben didn't want to see it, couldn't bear to see it, but he couldn't look away from it, while the huge, horrifying orc before him—laughed. Laughed, because wait, he'd been letting Eben watch this, letting him see how his intended target was so obviously enamoured with someone else.

"Ach, Tryggr is busy, I ken," the orc drawled, as Eben's blinking, traitorous eyes watched Tryggr's hips start plunging, while the orc beneath him gasped and moaned. "Thus, mayhap you can find other pleasures also, ach?"

Curse this orc, curse this horrible overwhelming room, this horrible day, the horrible sick jealousy screeching in Eben's belly. This had been so foolish, so, so foolish, *never trust a Skai, never let one get you alone*, but Eben had promised, he had, and he needed to fulfill his promise, and then run as fast as he could, until he could collapse a tunnel behind him...

"Tryggr!" he shouted, through his hoarse throat. "*Tryggr!* Help!"

9

For an instant, nothing happened. Nothing, but the incessant noise and chaos, while Tryggr kept plunging into the orc beneath him.

And the huge orc saw it, and laughed. Laughed, loud and triumphant, as he pinned Eben closer against the wall, his breath hot and nauseating, his swollen groin grinding hard into Eben's belly.

Eben's panic was screaming white and wild, now, blinding his eyes, trembling his entire body against the orc's massive bulk. What could he do, surely someone would notice or help, maybe he could catch Efterar or Kesst's attention somehow—but the room was too full of noise and blood and mayhem, oh please, please—

"Help!" Eben gasped. "Help, please! Please! *Sir!*"

When—there. Tryggr's body jerked up, his head snapping sideways, toward—toward Eben. Toward where Eben was cringing and cowering against the wall, against the orc—and oh no, no, Eben could even feel water streaking down his cheeks, hot and shameful and humiliating. While Tryggr just kept blankly staring at him, as if not seeing, not following. Maybe not even—not even caring.

And oh, Eben didn't care, he didn't, *never trust a Skai*, never—but wait. Wait. Tryggr was leaping to his feet, yanking up his trousers. And then lurching over toward them with astonishing speed, vaulting over another pair of grappling orcs on the way.

"What the fuck, Skaap!" Tryggr snarled, as he drove his shoulder into the huge orc, and shoved him sideways. "Can't you scent how terrified he is? Skai-kesh above, he's *weeping*!"

And no, no, Eben wasn't weeping, why was he weeping, the water streaming down his face, his head hanging, his shoulders heaving. Betraying all his shame, his horrifying humiliation, for all these orcs to see, for this Skaap to see, for Tryggr to see—

"Ach, Ka-esh," came Tryggr's voice, rushed and urgent—and that was his hand on Eben's face, tilting it up toward him. "Ach, you're all right. I've got you. Naught to fear, ach?"

Oh. *Oh.* Eben sank against the wall behind him, his eyes fluttering closed, and that was an odd sound from Tryggr before him, much like a growl—but his hand kept cradling Eben's face, caressing against his wet cheek. "Ach, naught to fear, sweet Ka-esh. No need to scent thus. Skaap shall *never* come near you again."

His voice had deepened at the end, into something hard and almost dangerous—and when Eben blinked up again, Tryggr was baring his teeth, and glaring over his shoulder. Toward where a cold-eyed Skaap was rapidly backing away from them, sinking into the clamouring throng.

It was enough to sag Eben heavier against the wall, and perhaps he'd even managed a nod. And Tryggr's hand on his face gave another approving little caress, his eyes slowly softening, despite the grim tightness still on his mouth.

"You're all right, Ka-esh," he said, even gentler than before.

"Now, is aught else amiss? You come here to find me? To speak to me?"

Eben twitched another nod, and suddenly the urgent surging panic was here again, stark and scraping in his belly. "It's—Alma," he gasped. "She's—gone. Run away."

Tryggr's eyes snapped wide, and then darted sideways, catching on—Drafli. Drafli, halfway across the room, his lean body whirling through the air, and hurling another orc onto the floor. But he'd almost seemed to sense Tryggr's gaze, somehow, because he twitched around, frowning—and then Tryggr's hand rapidly began moving in midair, speaking in their sign language.

Drafli instantly stiffened, his hand snatching sideways, toward—oh. Baldr, who'd been fighting close beside him. And at another sharp motion from Drafli's clawed hand, Baldr frowned and closed his eyes, inhaling deep—and then he stiffened all over, too. And without a word, or a single glance around them, they both sprinted for the door, dodging and leaping over other orcs as they went.

"I'd best round up a few brothers to help, just in case," Tryggr said now, turning back to Eben with unmistakable urgency in his scent. "Mayhap you oughta—"

He hesitated, grimacing and glancing around the still-chaotic room—but at least that terrifying Skaap orc was no longer in sight, and Eben drew in a thick, shaky breath. "I shall go," he replied, as steadily as he could. "I hope Alma shall soon—be found, and safe."

Tryggr twitched a nod, and that was distinct relief in his eyes. Wanting Eben well out of the way, clearly, and Eben fought to ignore the plunge in his belly as he took another breath, and shoved himself sideways. Lurching back along the wall toward the exit—which suddenly seemed very far away—and his panic was already rattling higher, his eyes darting around at the utter chaos of this horrible room. He could only push himself through it, hope no one else would notice him, and...

And then something grasped his hand, warm and firm—and when Eben startled to look, it was only Tryggr again, an apologetic smile on his mouth. "I'll walk you out, Ka-esh," he said. "Naught to fear, ach?"

Eben couldn't deny the sudden sinking relief, heavily dropping his shoulders, even as more bitter, shameful misery churned in his belly. Tryggr had seen his fear, and was now coddling him, condescending to him, as though Eben were some helpless, useless weakling, a *pet*, who couldn't cross a room unattended. And worst of all, it was true, and Eben desperately clung to that solid warm hand as Tryggr began striding toward the door, drawing Eben swiftly along behind him.

To Eben's relief, they reached the corridor without further incident, though the scent of Tryggr's urgency was now burning through the air—so Eben squared his shoulders, and withdrew his hand as quickly as he could. "Th-thank you," he said. "I wish you—all speed."

Tryggr nodded, and flashed Eben a brief, distracted smile—and then he spun around and away, disappearing back into the chaos of the room. While Eben just stood there outside the door, blinking hard, as his stomach twisted with more sinking, staggering misery. This had been so, so pathetic. So foolish. What had he been thinking, to have ever imagined he could—well. *Never trust a Skai. Never let one touch you, or get you alone...*

The sickening vision of Skaap was now churning with all the rest, the lingering scent of his breath still far too strong in Eben's nose, and he forced his shaky feet to move, away. Away, away, as far as he could go, as deep as he could go, where no Skai would ever find him again.

10

E ben ended up bloody and bent-over in the *dýflissa*, gasping and shivering and begging for more. Offering it up to any orc who wanted it, any orc who would fill him, flay him, force him to forget.

And though it was pain, and perhaps more humiliation, Eben couldn't stop. Couldn't bear to be empty, to lose that raw, reassuring certainty of a strong, hard prick plunged deep inside him. He was safe, like this. He was already full, already in pain. And despite how it looked, how it felt, there was still the awareness, low and fundamental, that he was still in control. If he wanted it to stop, it would, and every Ka-esh in the room would defend this, and hurl the offending orc out at once. Eben still held the power. The right to do this, to be this, to be a foolish, weeping orc who could take a half-dozen loads, and keep begging for more.

"Mayhap you ought to rest for a spell, Eben," a breathless Gareth finally said, once he'd emptied himself for the second time, and had begun gently licking at the fresh wounds on Eben's burning, aching back. "These are not healing as they should, ach?"

Eben's rebellion surged up before he could stop it, escaping in a low growl from his mouth—but Gareth just kept licking, kissing, even as his claws sank into Eben's hips. Knowing full well that Eben had never been able to refuse that heady, perfect blend of pain and tenderness, and Eben was already wilting beneath it, sagging weakly against the wall before him. And perhaps finally feeling the true extent of that pain, blaring across his back, and still coiling deep and despairing in his belly.

Foolish. Never trust a Skai.

"Come, then," came Gareth's low, soothing voice, as he nudged something soft—Eben's abandoned trousers—into his slack hand. "Rest for a spell, and come back tomorrow, if you yet need this relief."

Eben couldn't find the will to argue, and he suddenly felt so, so tired, worn and ragged and aching all over. And even putting on his trousers was far too difficult, and he was distantly, fervently grateful for Gareth's firm hand on his arm, holding him upright. And once Eben had finally managed it, Gareth pulled on his own trousers, passed Eben his tunic—which he would otherwise have fully forgotten—and guided him toward the door.

Eben went without looking, without scenting, with only more deep, dragging gratefulness toward Gareth, and a vague nattering dread of how much he would regret this tomorrow. And it wasn't until they were in the corridor that he suddenly scented something. Something that didn't at all belong, and Eben's breath drew in, his bleary eyes snapping open, and finding—

Tryggr. Tryggr, standing here in the Ka-esh corridor, and staring at him.

Eben froze all over, alarm screeching through his chest—Skai never came here, he was supposed to be safe here. And curse him, he wasn't wearing his tunic, and even if Tryggr hadn't been able to scent the fresh blood and seed all over Eben's tired, trembling body, he now had a full-on view of it, his eyes narrowing as they rapidly ran up and down Eben's torso. And then shifting even darker as they darted toward Gareth, who was still holding Eben by the elbow.

"Who the hell are you?" Tryggr snapped at Gareth, his voice sharper than Eben had yet heard it. "An' where are you taking him?"

Eben blinked, as more confused alarm juddered through his exhausted body, but beside him, Gareth stayed solid and steady, without even a trace of fear in his scent. "I am Gareth— or oft, Gary," he replied mildly. "And I am only taking him to his room."

Tryggr's narrow gaze snapped back to Eben, as if wanting him to confirm the accuracy of this claim—and somehow, Eben nodded. Nodded, holding his wide eyes to Tryggr's, needing him to understand, to agree. And he was vaguely surprised to see Tryggr's eyes softening in return, his swallow bobbing in his throat.

"Ach, I see," he said thickly, as he ran a hand against his bound-back hair. "Didn't mean to interrupt. I'll leave you be, then, Ka-esh, and find you another time."

He was already backing away, about to leave, no, no—and Eben lurched forward, out of Gareth's grip. "Wait," he croaked, as a hazy awareness finally whirled in his brain, because Tryggr had to have news, right? "Is Alma well? Did they bring her back?"

Tryggr's gaze had again darted sideways, toward Gareth— who was already backing toward the *dýflissa*, his hands upraised. "Only call if you need me, brother," he said to Eben, a little too smoothly. "And sleep well, ach?"

Eben rapidly nodded, and couldn't help a grateful, genuine smile toward him, and a quick wave farewell. But once he turned back to Tryggr again, he found him still looking decidedly unsettled, and frowning darkly at where Gareth had gone.

"Is aught—amiss, then?" Eben croaked, into the stilted silence, as the alarm shuddered back through his chest. "Is Alma lost? Or harmed?"

Tryggr's lean body twitched, his gaze snapping back to Eben's face—and again, brief but unmistakable, down to his bare, sweaty, bloody chest. "No, they found her," he said, on a heavy exhale. "She's back in the sickroom now, and Boss is with her. He's gonna make her an offer, I ken, to make sure she stays put, where we can keep an eye on her. Not safe for her to be running about thus, ach?"

Eben couldn't even pretend to hide the surprise in his scent—Drafli was now going to make Alma an *offer*, to keep her here? To keep her safe, after all that? But there was again no trace of guile in Tryggr's scent, and it distantly occurred to Eben that if Drafli truly still wanted Alma dead, it would have been far easier to let her keep running, and then to stage some convenient accident afterwards... right?

Never trust a Skai, the voice was droning again, but Tryggr was still here, shifting on his feet, and thrusting something into Eben's arms. Something Eben hadn't even noticed him carrying, and when he blinked downwards, he found himself holding a small cloth sack, full of—fresh *fruit*?

"An' just—wanted to be sure you were—all good," Tryggr said, with a grimace. "Didn't feel right, leaving you how I did. 'Specially after you went outta your way to help, and find me, even after that scum Skaap—"

He broke off there, glowering beyond Eben up the corridor, his hands flexing at his sides. "Reported him to Boss and Simon, by the way, after a chat with my Pa," he said flatly. "The clan's gonna deal with him, ach?"

Something swerved in Eben's belly, because oh, Tryggr hadn't truly done that, for *him*? But wait, curse it, Eben didn't want to cause any trouble, either. Didn't want to be responsible for any kind of retaliation whatsoever, and what if this Skaap decided to take it out on Eben, or gain revenge, or—or—

But wait, Tryggr had lurched closer, and clasped his hand to Eben's shoulder. "Naught to fear, Ka-esh," he said, low and firm. "It's got naught now to do with you, and we just don't want it to happen again, ach? We can't have it being dangerous for someone to come bring us an urgent message, affecting our own kin. Boss never woulda forgiven himself if that woman had come to harm running alone out there, ach? Most of all if he'd known you were trying to get word to him, but couldn't, because you got attacked by a so-called brother instead."

His eyes on Eben's had darkened again, his hand tightening on his shoulder. "It was good of you, Ka-esh," he said, low. "Good of you, and brave as hell, too. You ever even walk in that arena before? Or witness a proper brawl?"

Eben shook his head, betraying a faint wince, because again, it was so weak, so foolish, he was supposed to be a medic, wasn't he? "N-not—thus," he confessed. "I mean—I have attended skirmishes and battlefields, afterwards, to offer care when it is needed. But I have never been sent into—the full midst of this."

And truly, it was a gift that the war with men had been over for most of Eben's time as a medic, because what would he have done, if he'd needed to go straight into a pitched battle? What would he have done if Efterar had even decided to send him into that arena, rather than going himself?

"Well, we're grateful, Ka-esh," Tryggr said, his eyes flinty on Eben's face. "You didn't need to do it, and you did it anyway, even when it couldn'a been easy for you. When it coulda *harmed* you."

An odd ripple snaked up Eben's spine, and he swallowed, attempted a smile. "I was glad to help," he said thickly. "And I am—quite all right, of course."

But Tryggr's eyes had again flicked down Eben's front, toward the sweat and scratches and blood. Almost as clear as if he'd spoken his doubt aloud, and Eben drew in breath, cleared his throat. "This was just—for pleasure," he said, with a vague, shaky wave toward the *dýflissa* up the corridor. "Ka-esh oft do this, for it is an easy way to clear one's thoughts, and forget—"

But wait, curse him, why was he saying this, betraying this, before this orc, of all orcs—but it was too late, and that was far too much awareness, shifting across Tryggr's watching eyes. "Seems like a lot to forget, though, if it takes what, eight orcs to do it?" he asked, his voice light. "An' what's this from, a lash?"

His claw had very lightly reached to touch Eben's chest, brushing against—Eben's wide eyes darted downwards—oh. Where the whip had very clearly curled around his torso, and drawn a vivid line against his skin, still seeping dark red blood. And wait, was Tryggr judging him, and had it really been eight orcs, and Tryggr could smell that, and—

The humiliation burned up into Eben's face, roiling hard and sick in his belly, and he needed to leave, needed to escape, run as deep as he could—but Tryggr's other hand was still clasping his shoulder, holding him here, where he could judge him, and mock him. And all that was left was for Eben to force his face up, to hold his blinking, miserable eyes to Tryggr's face.

"As if you have any right to judge me?" his thin voice demanded, harsh in his throat. "How many weakened orcs do you take in that arena, or mayhap in the corridors, once you have gained their defeat?"

He knew it was unfair even as he spoke it, but the sickness and exhaustion were still curdling in his belly, his vision flooded with images of Tryggr laughing with that Skai orc, pinning him down, driving his scarred swollen prick into him with such smooth, confident ease. And Eben wasn't jealous, he was *not*, and—

And wait, Tryggr was reeling backwards, away, his

expression stunned, almost hurt. "This has naught to do with their defeat," he hissed back. "It's only what *Skai* oft do, when *we* wish for release. And I ken it's better than running a blood-soaked *rut* upon a weak small Ka-esh, and wielding a *lash* against him, when he's yet *reeking* of fear and despair!"

Oh. Oh, no. No, no, no. *A weak small Ka-esh. Reeking of fear and despair.* And the pain cracking through Eben's chest was far worse than his stinging back, or his aching, burning arse. He couldn't bear to let Tryggr see him weep, not again, please, please—

But Tryggr was seeing it, he was staring at Eben with more judgement in his eyes, and with something almost like—like contempt. Contempt toward Eben, for his size, his weakness, his fear, his despair...

Never trust a Skai, his father's grating voice shouted, *run as deep as you can*—and this time, Eben was listening. Listening, weeping, as he whirled away, covered his face, and ran.

11

Eben spent an endless, miserable night.

It took far too long to fall asleep, what with his leaking eyes, and the ever-increasing aches running through his weakened, exhausted body. Aches that eventually began to feel more like chills, and it belatedly occurred to his weary, overwhelmed brain that perhaps Gareth—and Tryggr—had been right. Perhaps he'd pushed it too far in the *dýflissa*. He'd had far too little sleep these past days, and beyond that apple Tryggr had thrown him, he couldn't recall if he'd eaten the day before, either—and curse him, he hadn't thought to drink even a bit of fresh seed in the *dýflissa*, either. Orc healing never worked as well when the orc was fatigued or under-nourished, or—Eben groaned into his fur—or under strain.

So he attempted to lie still, to rest, and eventually pulled over that sack of fruit Tryggr had given him, which he'd somehow carried all the way here. But he suddenly felt too weary to even eat it, and instead ended up sucking out a plum's juices as well as he could before collapsing again. His body still shivering with wave after wave of cold, though the fur beneath him was soaked with sweat, and his back felt like it was fully aflame, licking and crackling with agonizing heat.

Eventually he fell into a fitful, restless sleep, and when he awoke again, he was parched, the wet fur now frigid against his shivering skin. But he was too weak to get out of bed, and there was no water to be found, so he finally groped for another plum, and again sucked as much liquid from it as he could. And then sank his trembling body back onto the bed, fighting to ignore the distant shouting awareness that he was feverish, and that the whip-strikes had clearly become infected. *These are not healing as they should...*

Eben didn't know when he next awoke, but when he did, it was to the sound of a low, cursing voice. A familiar voice. And Eben had to be dreaming, dreaming that Tryggr was in his room, and yes, no, the scent was gone again—until it wasn't. And with it was another familiar scent, Gareth's scent, but hanging thick with metal and smoke, suggesting he'd just come from his work in the forge.

"How long's he been like this?" demanded Tryggr's voice. "An' why the fuck did none of you come check on him? Didn't you scent him, the other night, when you were tearing into him with a fucking *lash*, after he near got attacked and *forced* in the fucking Skai arena?!"

The sharp scent of Gareth's shock filtered through the air, and Eben could hear his low, hoarse exhale. "Ach, he spoke naught of this," he replied, his voice sounding odd to Eben's ears. "And he oft comes scenting thus, and begging for pain. And if I—or another friend—do not grant him this, he shall hurl himself toward any other who shall offer it. Oft those who shall not pay close heed to him, or his scents."

Oh. No. Gareth truly didn't think such things about Eben, he truly hadn't taken pleasure with Eben out of *pity*, or a sense of *responsibility*, all this time?! And it was surely a sign of Eben's miserable state that his sudden guilt and grief didn't even filter into his scent, at least not enough to reach Tryggr and Gareth beside him.

"And I only did not come to see him," continued Gareth's voice, still thick and unusually high-pitched, "because I thought—your scents—I thought he had gone with *you.*"

There was an instant's silence, taut and heavy in the room, and a sound from Gareth that might have been a sniff. And then the sound of movement, of perhaps Tryggr pacing, his scent swaying unevenly into Eben's breath. "Then where are those pricks from the sickroom, those ones he works with!" Tryggr demanded. "Those Ash-Kai always got their noses poked in everyone else's business, and that mouthy one Kesst kept launching right into me for even *asking* about Boss's woman! Why ain't he down here gettin' his magic healer mate to deal with this!"

There was another moment's silence, broken by Gareth's heavy-sounding sigh. "Outside the *dýflissa*, he is not one to draw eyes to himself," his quiet voice said. "He is so meek and soft-spoken, I ken he is mayhap easy to... forget. Most of all in such a busy sickroom, ach?"

His words were followed by more uncomfortable silence, and a harsh, irritated growl from Tryggr. "So what's keeping you from running for Efterar now, then!" he snarled. "When *you're* part responsible for putting him in this state!"

There was a flare of bright alarm from Gareth, but then Eben could scent him rushing from the room, leaving only Tryggr's scent behind. And now something heavy was settling on the bed beside Eben, something warm and familiar touching his shoulder.

"Ach, you'll be all right, Ka-esh," came Tryggr's low voice. "You'll be all right real soon, ach? You've been real good to keep resting like this, real good."

Oh. Eben attempted to turn his head toward Tryggr, to blink his gritty eyes open, perhaps to speak—but nothing would come out. And despite that, Tryggr's warm hand had begun stroking his shoulder, slow and deeply reassuring, and Eben couldn't help curling a little closer into him, into his safe solid warmth.

"That's it, Ka-esh," Tryggr's soft voice continued. "You just relax and breathe, ach? That Efterar will be here real soon to help you, I ken."

Eben might have nodded, curling even closer, his head bumping something solid—something that was now shifting, slipping beneath his head, propping it up. And wait, wait, it was Tryggr's *thigh*, Eben's head was in Tryggr's *lap*—and Tryggr's warm hand was now stroking against his hair, against where it felt sticky and scraggly, surely half fallen out of its usual neat braid.

"Ach, just thus, Ka-esh," Tryggr said, even softer. "You get comfortable, and rest."

Eben somehow nodded, rubbing his hot cheek against the rough fabric of Tryggr's trousers, but oh, this was the best he'd felt in days, or maybe in weeks, or months. Just lying like this in a Skai's lap, while the Skai kept petting him, murmuring soft, sweet, wonderful words to him.

Eben didn't know how long he lay there, and he'd perhaps fallen back asleep—but he was jolted awake by Tryggr's voice again, now far louder and sharper than before. "Where the fuck have *you* been?" he demanded, and when Eben's scratchy eyes blinked open, he saw Efterar striding into the room, looking just as bleary and exhausted as Eben felt.

"I've been dealing with the fallout from that massive brawl of yours, Skai," Efterar snapped back, though Eben couldn't taste any actual ire in his scent. "Now help me turn him over, will you? *Gently.*"

Efterar was referring to Eben, he soon discovered, as careful hands shifted against his body, turning him around so his burning back faced out, toward Efterar. Which meant that

Eben's face was now turned toward Tryggr, his nose nearly in Tryggr's groin, and he felt himself reflexively inhaling the rich sweet scent of it, as his aching body shuddered all over.

"Ach, that's a bad infection," said Efterar's voice, clipped and businesslike. "What did it, do you know?"

Tryggr's hand was again steadily stroking Eben's hair, seemingly not caring that it was nudging Eben's face closer into his groin. "A lash, he said," came Tryggr's flat reply. "An' a half-dozen fool greedy Ka-esh running a rut on him, too. Thought they were s'posed to be the geniuses round here."

Efterar didn't make any comment to this, though Eben could feel the unmistakable prickle of his powerful healing magic, shimmering into the aches on his skin. "He's badly dehydrated, too," said Efterar's matter-of-fact voice. "Lost a lot of blood. I don't suppose you thought to bring him any water, beyond this fruit?"

Tryggr's hand stilled, and Eben could feel his breath hissing out, hard enough to rustle his hair. "Ach, no, I didn't," he breathed. "Fuck. I shoulda thought of it. Didn't realize he didn't have any, the poor little pet."

Another hard shiver hurtled up Eben's back, and he could hear Efterar's low harrumph. "Well, fresh seed would be even better, if you'd want to give it," he said flatly. "No obligation whatsoever, of course, but it scents to me like you're both already halfway there."

Wait. Wait, what the hell had Efterar just said, and Eben couldn't stop shivering now, and somehow—somehow—twisting his head a little, and blinking up at Tryggr's face. At where Tryggr was blinking back down toward him, a stunned, strange look shifting across his eyes.

"Would that help, Ka-esh?" he asked, hoarse. "A bit of fresh seed? Just—for your health? Your healing?"

Right. Right, of course, just for that, and Eben couldn't deny his low, shaky moan, his tongue brushing his lips. And now he was even inhaling slow and deep, shamefully nuzzling his face into Tryggr's groin, into where—at some point—it had begun bulging far larger than before.

"Ach, then, Ka-esh," Tryggr breathed, and oh, *oh*, he was shifting his trousers, tugging them downwards, and releasing— that. That fat, scarred Skai prick, hovering huge and heavy over Eben's face. And this was not happening, this could not be happening, not with Efterar right there behind them—but Eben knew Efterar had witnessed such feedings hundreds of times, and he'd been the one to suggest it, and...

"Ach, Ka-esh?" Tryggr said, even as he shifted Eben a little on his lap, lowered that thick grey length toward Eben's mouth. "You're sure?"

But Eben's mouth was still watering, his head furtively nodding, his face seeking closer. His lips parting, opening, welcoming the gentle brush of that slick grey head, its seed brushing lightly across his tongue...

Fuck, it tasted good, different, richer and sweeter than any seed Eben had ever tasted in his life—and he moaned as he lurched closer, sucked it deeper into his mouth. While Tryggr gasped above him, and then huffed a husky laugh, his hand again stroking against Eben's hair, claws gently dragging against his scalp.

"Ach, there you are, Ka-esh," Tryggr murmured, as his cock in Eben's mouth shuddered and swelled larger, squeezing out a generous pulse of that rich sweetness onto Eben's tongue. "That's better, ain't it?"

Eben briefly, fervently nodded, earning another low laugh from Tryggr, another stroke of claws through his hair. "Good," he said softly. "Real good, Ka-esh. Drink as much as you like."

Oh, hell, and Eben moaned again, sucking harder, deeper—and that was a hiss from Tryggr this time. "Ach, that's it," he breathed, swelling even fuller in Eben's mouth, stretching it wider around him. "Ach, you've got a tight, hot little mouth, don't you? You like having it filled with a good Skai prick?"

Eben's groan was hoarse, shameless, his mouth sucking even harder—and oh, it felt good, it tasted good, and perhaps it really was helping, too. Because Efterar's familiar healing prickle in his back was moving faster now, darting efficiently from laceration to laceration, and Eben's thoughts felt clearer, his body steadier. Enough that he remembered his tongue, flicking and teasing it at Tryggr's leaking slit, while Tryggr spasmed and sputtered into his mouth, thicker and smoother with every desperate gulp.

"Good, Ka-esh," Tryggr gasped, his clawed hand now gently curling around Eben's neck, his breaths heaving loud and harsh. "Ach, that's nice. Real nice. So good and tight and sweet, so pretty with a Skai in your mouth, opening you up, about to make you reek of—"

His voice faltered, broke into a hoarse, guttural cry—and yes, yes, there it was, the furious rush of sweet, stunning Skai seed, surging into Eben's mouth. And he was aware enough now to soften the suction, to open his throat, to just let the seed flow straight down, heating his esophagus, streaming into his empty waiting belly.

"Oh, *fuck*," Tryggr groaned, his hooded eyes bright and wild on Eben's face. "So *good*, Ka-esh. *Ach*."

Eben could have preened beneath the praise, beneath the sheer sweeping pleasure, the wondrous warm rightness of this powerful Skai so generously filling his mouth, flooding his belly. Offering him such great, stunning strength, and Eben held his worshipful eyes on Tryggr's flushed face as he kept his throat wide open, kept welcoming that sweet Skai seed inside him. Until he could feel the flow finally sputtering, slowing, and only then did he let his throat convulse against that hard invading flesh, even as his tongue stroked up its length. An action that instantly made Tryggr shudder and gasp, squeezing out another sustained spurt of seed—so Eben did it again, and again. Milking out more and more, squeezing again and again, until that slowly softening cock had fed him every last, succulent drop.

"Ach, Ka-esh," Tryggr breathed, or perhaps it was more a moan, as he bent over Eben's head, and inhaled slow and deep. "Ach, that was good. So tight. So *sweet*."

Eben softly drew away and smiled back up at him, his breath slowly shuddering with his exhale, with his heavy, fluttering eyes. The peacefulness now settling quiet and boneless upon him, sinking him down into the warm safety of Tryggr's lap, his still-stroking hands. Liking him, approving of him, perhaps, perhaps...

"That better, Ka-esh?" breathed Tryggr's ragged voice. "Now mayhap you can sleep for me, ach?"

And yes, yes, Eben would, he would like nothing better than to please his lord, who had blessed him with such good seed, and such great kindness. So he kept smiling as he nodded, slow and grateful, and then closed his eyes, and slept.

12

When Eben fully awoke again, he was alone in his bed.

There was a bulging waterskin beside him, and the sack of fruit appeared to have been replenished—and he had vague memories of Efterar speaking to him, touching his back, pouring bottles of Eben's own tonic down his throat.

If you don't mind, I'd like to keep you here resting for a few days, Ka-esh, Efterar's voice had said. *It feels like you haven't slept in a week, and you need the time to heal. You've done more than enough work lately.*

Eben had been too exhausted to argue, though he did recall searching for Tryggr, and finding a fresh trace of his scent, as if he'd recently been in the room. And it had been enough to lull Eben back to sleep again, sinking into the memories of it, the faint sweet taste of Tryggr on his tongue.

And even now, as Eben carefully shoved himself up in his bed, drawing in a slow breath, he could still *taste* Tryggr. Could still taste that distinct Skai sweetness not only on his lips, but in his own scent, in his flesh, embedded stark and powerful beneath his very skin.

He'd sucked off a Skai. A *Skai*.

Even the thought of it swarmed heat up Eben's spine, and deep into his already-swelling groin. *Good. Real good. Ach, you've got a tight, hot little mouth, don't you? You like having it filled with a good Skai prick?*

Fuck. It was as though Tryggr had struck straight to Eben's deepest, most fundamental cravings, without even the slightest effort. The easy commands. The praise. The claws in his hair, on his neck. The way Tryggr had looked, the way he'd gasped. As if, in that moment, he'd truly wanted Eben. As if he'd... cared.

But Tryggr wasn't here... now. He hadn't... stayed. But in truth, why would he? Because he'd only done that for Eben's health, right? There had been no other commitments, no agreements between them whatsoever—and even if Tryggr had found pleasure in it, that didn't mean anything, did it? That never meant anything, not among their kin, and especially not among the Skai. *Never trust a Skai.*

That thought hitched uncomfortably in Eben's chest, and he forced himself up and out of bed, staggering on shaky legs over to the nearby latrine. Where he washed up all over, brushing and braiding his hair, before dressing in a fresh tunic and trousers, and finally heading up to the sickroom.

His heartbeat pounded louder as he went, his traitorous breaths inhaling slow and deep. Seeking any hints of Tryggr's scent in the adjacent corridors or rooms, any suggestions he might have recently come this way—but there was no fresh trace of him, not in the Ka-esh wing, or the Grisk. Or—Eben couldn't deny the miserable plunge in his belly as he hesitated in the doorway—the sickroom.

Kesst and Alma weren't in the sickroom, either—or Salvi, due to his trip north. There was only Efterar, working on the other side of the room, and a variety of new Bautul and Skai patients, no doubt from that vicious brawl in the arena. Which now must have been multiple days ago, and Eben's scattering thoughts were fixed on the memory of Tryggr pinning that Skai orc down, sliding so easy inside him—

"Good to see you up again, Ka-esh," interrupted a familiar voice, and Eben blinked at where Efterar was now striding over, his eyes still red and heavy with exhaustion. "Feeling better, I hope?"

Eben nodded, and cleared his throat. "Yes, much better, thank you," he replied thickly. "It was good of you to come and see me."

Efterar waved it away, even as he reached around, and hovered his hand up and down over Eben's back. "Glad to help," he said. "Though you should still take it easy over the next week or two. Cut down your time working in here, and *rest*. Also"—he grimaced, as Eben felt a distinctive prickle in one of the mostly healed cuts—"I'm sorry I didn't catch your absence sooner. That Skai was very unimpressed with me."

There was an apologetic half-smile on his face, and Eben's heart pounded faster, a hot shudder streaking up his spine. "Have you—seen Tryggr?" he asked, before he could stop himself. "Or scented him, since then?"

Curse him, what was he saying, or betraying, but Efterar surely knew, Efterar had watched him desperately sucking Tryggr's prick, hadn't he? But thankfully, Efterar hadn't seemed to notice anything unusual about Eben's question, and he gave a distracted-looking shrug, his focus still fixed on Eben's back.

"Ach, he's been by a few times," he replied absently. "Recently tore a knee ligament, fighting in the arena."

Wait. Wait. Eben's body had suddenly turned to ice, his hands clenching, his eyes staring at nothing. Tryggr had already gone back to that arena. To do what Skai often did, he'd said, when they wished for release. To do, perhaps, what Eben had witnessed him doing the other day, laughing and snapping his teeth as he'd sunk deep inside...

But curse it, even if Tryggr had fucked a dozen orcs since then, what right did Eben have to care? He knew it hadn't meant anything. He *knew*. Tryggr was clearly a kind, considerate orc, who made a point of helping those in need. So when Eben had been in need, Tryggr had done what he could to help. And then he'd had every right to move on with his life, with his activities, and his pleasures.

And that was all. That had to be all. It hadn't meant anything. *Never trust a Skai.*

But it made for another long, lonely, empty day. And though Eben threw himself into work—briefing himself on all the new patients, updating their charts, refreshing bandages, prescribing and preparing and distributing tonic and herbs as needed—it didn't seem to help, or to keep his brain from wheeling back toward Tryggr again and again. It hadn't meant anything, it hadn't...

Eben worked late into the night again, his exhaustion growing heavier and heavier with every breath. And when a trace of a succulent, overpowering scent flared into his nostrils, he didn't even look up. Just kept crushing his herbs, squeezing his eyes shut, he was exhausted and imagining things, and that was all—

"Aren't you s'posed to be resting, Ka-esh?" asked a voice, low, familiar, far too close. And when Eben's eyes snapped open, it was—*Tryggr*. Tryggr, standing here beside his workbench, and looking at him.

Eben nearly dropped the pestle he'd been holding—Tryggr was *here*—but somehow he caught it again, and set it down with a clatter. "Oh," he croaked, and he couldn't help his inhale, dragging in the sweet, stunning scent swarming through the air. "I—I did rest. A lot."

Tryggr cocked a brow, as a wry smile pulled at his mouth. "Thing about resting, though," he said, "is that you gotta keep doing it, Ka-esh."

His voice was mild, but Eben could still feel the faint twinge of reprimand beneath it, and he couldn't suppress his reflexive wince, or his fervent, awkward nod. While Tryggr just kept looking at him, shifting on his feet, something moving in his eyes that Eben couldn't at all read.

"Healing all right, though?" Tryggr asked now, a little gruff. "An' you haven't gone back for any more ruts or lashings, have you?"

Eben winced again, and gripped his shaky, sweaty hands at the solid wood of the workbench. "N-no," he gulped. "N-not yet."

And wait, why had he said that, it sounded like he was *planning* to go back to the *dýflissa*—was he?—and he shook his head, opened his mouth. But nothing came out, and Tryggr's eyes shifted again, his arms smoothly folding over his chest.

"Well, take it easy in there next time, ach?" he said coolly. "Not much relief if it brings you real harm, is it? An' keeps you running back for more?"

Eben's wince felt like a flinch this time, and he couldn't help his reflexive glance downwards, toward Tryggr's legs. Because Efterar had said he'd torn a ligament fighting in the arena, hadn't he? And yes, yes, Tryggr was clearly favouring his left knee, betraying a faint hiss as he again shifted on his feet.

"M-mayhap I could say the—the same," Eben's hoarse voice stammered. "About the—the arena."

And curse him, *curse* him, because that was disbelief flaring across Tryggr's eyes, followed by a sudden, dark disapproval. "Not the same, Ka-esh," he snapped. "The arena's part of my *job*. We train to keep kin like you Ka-esh *safe*. To *help* you."

Oh. Part of his job, helping orcs like Eben. Weak orcs, Tryggr meant, foolish orcs, orcs who got themselves needlessly injured in the *dýflissa*, and therefore required impromptu feedings for their health. And of course it didn't mean anything, it had never meant anything, Eben had been dreaming, delirious, *never trust a Skai...*

"I know," he finally whispered, his voice cracking, his prickling eyes dropping to the workbench, to the mess of herbs he'd somehow made upon it. "I am s-sorry, sir."

There was a moment's brief, horrible silence, during which Eben's lip began badly quivering, betraying him, no, no, no. And he was about to abandon it all, to rush past Tryggr to the door, when something grasped his arm. Something—oh. Tryggr's hand.

Eben's fearful eyes darted up, blinking at where Tryggr was grimacing, and running his other hand against his hair. "No need to apologize, Ka-esh," he said, a little rushed. "Didn't mean to snap at you. It's just"—he grimaced again, shook his head—"I busted this knee in there the other day, and it's making me ornery, ach? Boss took me off duty scouting, and he's had me resting and doing rubbish jobs ever since. Says starting tomorrow, he's putting me to work helping his woman in the *scullery* instead. Doing *laundry* and shit."

Wait. Amidst all this, Eben had almost entirely forgotten about Alma and her plight—and she hadn't shown up in the sickroom all day, had she? Was that because—she'd gone to work in the scullery? And Drafli was now sending Tryggr to *help* her? Doing *laundry*?!

"Is Alma—well?" Eben asked, his voice a croak. "Well enough to be—doing laundry?"

Tryggr shot Eben a look he couldn't all read, and then abruptly released his grip on Eben's arm. "Guess so," he said, without enthusiasm. "Though I s'pose I'll be the one to keep an eye on her again to make sure, ach?"

Right. Because that was Tryggr's job, and that was all. Keeping weak kin safe. To the point where Drafli had ordered him to do it, and...

"And Drafli still truly wishes to... help Alma?" Eben asked, before he could stop it. "And have her... stay?"

His tired brain was belatedly dredging up the last he'd heard about this, when Tryggr had suggested that Drafli might make Alma an offer, to keep her close and safe. And Tryggr twitched a nod, though something sharp and strangely bitter flared through his scent, and his eyes shifted past Eben, narrowing on the wall behind his head.

"Ach, Boss made her the offer," Tryggr said flatly. "Got her a room of her own in the Grisk wing, gave her plenty of goods and credits—and then he took her to bed with him and his mate, too. Covered her all over with their scents, made sure she found joy in it."

Wait. Truly? Drafli had taken Alma to *bed*? With him, *and* Baldr? After he'd tried to *kill* her?

But Tryggr's face looked a little mulish, now, his nod decisive and firm. And blinking at him, Eben's longing was suddenly far too close, surging hard in his belly. Because what would it be like, to have a fierce, handsome Skai watching over you, giving you gifts, taking you to bed, making sure you found joy in it...

Tryggr was fully frowning now, his claws tapping at his biceps, his scent even sharper than before. And too late Eben realized he was just foolishly standing there staring, and reeking of hunger, or perhaps even jealousy.

"But," he croaked, before he even caught it, "Drafli still does not even... *like* Alma, ach? Or truly want her, in his bed, with his mate? Not after how she has come between him and Baldr, with the scent-bond?"

But Tryggr's frown only deepened, and he jerked a dismissive-looking shrug. "It hasn't been the best start, I ken," he said flatly. "But I'm told the woman's sweet and loyal, and a hard worker—and eager to please and obey in bed, too. All just as

Skai like best, ach? So if she can keep it up, show Boss she's worth his time, I ken he'll come around."

Oh. *Oh.* Sweet, and loyal. A hard worker. Eager to please and obey in bed. *All just as Skai like best...*

Eben's heart was erratically pounding again, his eyes still frozen on Tryggr's face. On where Tryggr's frown twisted, tightened, as he jerked a swift, limping step backwards. "Well, glad you're feeling better, Ka-esh," he said. "Best of luck with—not sleeping, I s'pose."

With that, he spun and strode for the door, his shoulders very straight, his steps lurching with his limp. And it wasn't until he'd vanished into the corridor that Eben realized it, recognized part of what had held him so caught, so transfixed, so foolish, that entire time.

Tryggr hadn't borne any other fresh scents. Not even after so many days, after he'd returned to the arena.

Tryggr had only scented of... *Eben.*

13

Tryggr had only scented of Eben.

The certainty shouted again and again through Eben's awareness as he finally dragged himself back to bed, and sank into a long, deep night's sleep. A sleep he'd unquestionably needed, and when he awoke, he felt far fresher, his thoughts far clearer than before.

Tryggr had been worried about him. Tryggr had wanted to make sure he was well. Tryggr had only scented of him. Of *him.*

But maybe—Eben's distant rational brain pointed out, as he washed and dressed—maybe it still meant nothing. Or even if it had, maybe he'd run Tryggr off entirely last night, with his exhaustion and his foolishness and his babbling. With how he'd implied he would soon return to the *dýflissa.*

And yes, that temptation still shimmered there, dark and low in Eben's belly—but the truth of Tryggr's scent was stronger. The truth of Tryggr's care, and his words. The way Tryggr had spoken of Alma, and of Dratli.

The woman seems sweet. Loyal. A hard worker, eager to please in bed. All just as Skai like best. So if she can keep it up, show Boss she's worth his time, I ken he'll come around....

Keep it up. Show him. *He'll come around.*

It meant something. It had to mean something. And Eben had to know. He had to try. He had to.

So instead of going straight to the sickroom, Eben first went for the scullery. Drawing in deep breaths as he strode through the corridors, through the Grisk wing, into the large, fragrant kitchen. Where he fought to ignore the odd glances from the silver-haired Ash-Kai and the frowning Skai working over the fire, and held his eyes on the open door of the small adjoining scullery up ahead.

Where—yes, yes—that was Tryggr's scent. Tryggr's scent, and another unfamiliar orc's, too. And when Eben halted in the scullery door, he found Tryggr kneeling over a washbasin, elbows-deep in soapy water, and blinking at him.

And Eben was blinking at Tryggr, too. At his wet-spattered bare chest, his strong, soapy forearms. The sheen of sweat across his forehead and high cheekbones, the long black strands of hair falling out of his topknot. All making him look more... vulnerable, somehow, more approachable, and perhaps even more appealing than before.

But most compelling of all was his scent. Hanging thick and heavy in the air, and still only tasting of... Eben.

"What is it, Ka-esh?" Tryggr finally said, into the dangling silence. "Looking for Alma? She's gone out for a spell, I ken."

Eben twitched and shook his head, and drew in a shaky breath. "I—" he began, tried again. "I only wished to ask if—if you might have any need for—help."

Tryggr's brows shot up, and then he glanced sideways, toward where—oh. Right. There was another orc, an older Skai, crawling out from where he'd apparently been under the counter. And as Eben blinked toward him, and then toward the counter—which held a towering pile of laundry— it occurred to him that the scullery still looked far cleaner than it had the last time he'd seen it, when he'd fixed that foul drain, and it had been overrun with ash and filth and vermin.

"Thanks, Ka-esh, but Duff's already helping with the laundry," Tryggr said, with a jerk of his head toward the older Skai, who was fully ignoring Eben, in favour of intently licking what scented like fresh blood from his fingers. "An' don't you already have work in the sickroom to do?"

Eben's stomach plummeted, his gaze dropping, and he gulped down a deep breath. A breath that filled his nostrils with more of Tryggr's scent, so unnaturally strong in this small stuffy room. A scent that still tasted of... Eben.

It was enough to raise Eben's eyes again, though his tooth bit hard at his wavering lip, and his clammy hands wiped at his trousers. "Ach, I do," he said, his voice hitching. "And I should never forego my work there, or our patients who need my help. But Efterar wished me to cut back my time there, and I only thought—if there was aught else a Ka-esh might help you with, such as—"

His eyes darted sideways, to where he could see the stone marking the nearest closed air-vent, and he edged toward it, and pulled it out with a shaky hand. Revealing the familiar cranking mechanism behind it, and after a few moments of squeaky turning, a rush of sweet fresh air poured through the vent and into the too-hot room.

"Wait, there's another vent?" Tryggr's sharp voice demanded, though it sounded distinctly relieved, too. "Thought there was only one, under the counter. How the hell'd you know that one was there?"

Eben shrugged, and gave a shaky wave of his hand. "They are marked the same in every room," he replied, slightly steadier than before. "There is another there"—he nodded toward the wall behind the Duff orc, and then up at the ceiling—"and there, I ken. Our fathers would not have built a scullery with only one vent, ach? This risks leaking tainted air into the kitchen, and spreading disease throughout all the mountain."

Tryggr was still staring at him, his arms immobile in the soapy water, while this Duff promptly turned around, and began poking at the vent Eben had pointed out behind him. But his hands were clearly arthritic, his frustration already jolting through the air, so Eben furtively went to join him, attempting a careful smile toward his wrinkled, reddening face.

"Ach, you near have it," he said softly. "Only twist, thus—ach, this is good. Once or twice more, I ken."

Duff obliged, turning the crank twice more—and he crowed aloud at the sudden blast of cool air in his face. But Eben winced, wrinkling his nose, because the scent behind also reeked of vermin—not only dung, but live mice too.

"Ach, it is infested," he told Duff. "It ought to be cleaned out, but—"

He cast an uneasy glance over his shoulder toward Tryggr, who hadn't wanted his help—but Tryggr was just watching, with a look Eben couldn't at all read in his eyes. While beside Eben, Duff was eagerly nodding, and waving him toward it. "Clean," he said flatly. "Get vermin *out*."

Eben couldn't argue with that—it was a genuine health hazard to have vermin living in a scullery—and he showed Duff how to release the vent's grate, and draw it out of the wall. And before Eben had even had a chance to look inside, Duff shot out a knobbly hand, grasped a live squirming mouse from inside the vent, and bit into its throat.

Eben blinked, but obligingly waited as Duff rapidly drained the mouse—cracking open its neck for good measure—before bending his silver head to peer longingly into the vent. "Other mice run off," he said mournfully. "Mayhap come back, if we put vent in again?"

Eben half-smiled and nodded, even as he glanced around, and went to collect a small shovel and a bucket. "Mayhap after we clean this out," he replied, with as much firmness as he could muster. "We should not wish to leave it there to fester for next time, ach?"

Thankfully, Duff didn't protest, and even helped Eben clean the vent with surprising enthusiasm. And while Tryggr had seemingly returned to his laundry-scrubbing behind them, Eben could almost feel him still listening, watching, his eyes prickling on Eben's back as he dumped the detritus down the scullery's ash chute, along with the drained mouse. Which, Duff sadly lamented, did not taste nearly as good as the rats.

"Ach?" Eben asked over his shoulder, as he scrubbed his hands in the sink, and then waved Duff toward it, too. "You ken, rats bear some properties that make them easier to digest, and thus may gain you more nutrients. Do you oft long for rats to eat?"

Duff fervently nodded as he washed his hands too, the scent of his hunger swirling into the air, and Eben considered that for another moment. "I ken you may need more of a specific nutrient, and this is why you crave this so strongly," he said thoughtfully. "I should be glad to bring you some of our tonics to try, should you wish? Most orcs like the taste very much, and some have fresh blood in them, also."

Duff looked cautiously intrigued by this, and behind them, Tryggr finally cleared his throat. "Can't see how it's not worth trying, Duff," he said firmly. "Thanks, Ka-esh."

Eben's face heated, but he smiled and waved it away. "I am happy to help," he said, and then twitched at the familiar words, at the way they caught and flared in Tryggr's eyes. And Tryggr wasn't washing again, was just kneeling there looking at Eben with something almost wolfish in his eyes, and Eben drew up to his full height, drew up his breath and his courage. He had to try.

Keep it up. Show him. He'll come around...

"I could help in—other ways, also," he said, too quickly. "I could"—his eyes darted downwards, toward the bloodstained tunic Tryggr was scrubbing—"bring some chalk powder, to help with stains. Or mayhap more lye, for soap. Or a solution to help keep the drain clean, and free of foul vapours that could harm you. Or harm Alma, who you are meant to watch over."

He was still speaking far too fast, his eyes wide and almost pleading on Tryggr's face. And oh, that was surely softness in Tryggr's eyes, in his rueful little half-smile, half-grimace.

"Ach, well, all right, then, Ka-esh," he said, husky. "We'll be glad to have you, I ken."

Eben couldn't help his sudden, relieved smile, beaming brightly down toward Tryggr's flushed face. And if he wasn't mistaken, Tryggr's hands fumbled the tunic in the water, his face gone slightly redder than before.

And it was something, it had to be something. And Eben's smile pulled even wider as he nodded, and drew in a deep breath of that sweet, succulent scent. Tasting of him. Only him.

"Thank you, sir," he said, to those watching, shifting eyes. "I shall do my best."

14

For the next few days, Eben did his very best. Keeping up with his most important work in the sickroom, while also offering whatever support he could in the scullery.

It made for more long, busy days, but somehow, they didn't seem nearly as exhausting as before. Perhaps because it meant Eben left the sickroom at a reasonable hour every afternoon, to ensure he could still catch Tryggr in the scullery—and more often than not, Tryggr would eventually send him away to supper, or to bed.

"Off with you, Ka-esh," he would say, with a militant glint in his eye. "You need rest, remember? Don't want you crashing like that again."

Eben hadn't once attempted to argue, and in truth, it was a strange, surprising relief to be told, to have all the doubts and obligations firmly snatched from his hands. And if he wasn't mistaken, Tryggr rather enjoyed having his orders obeyed, too—and he would watch intently as he waited for Eben's answer, his brows raised, his expression cool and assessing.

"Ach, I ken, sir," Eben would reply, reflexively putting his hand over his heart, in what he now knew was Skai sign language for *thank you.* "I shall return tomorrow."

He didn't think he imagined the satisfied hitch in Tryggr's scent—especially at being called *sir*—and even if Eben continued to read in his bedroom after supper, he could still almost hear Tryggr's voice, close and hot in his ear. *You need rest. Keep it up. Show him. He'll come around...*

So Eben dutifully went to bed, though he often needed to stroke himself off before he could fall asleep, gasping and arching as visions of a hungry scarred prick and sharp Skai claws pulsed behind his eyes. He hadn't returned to the *dýflissa* since that night he'd been injured, and while he still longingly hesitated each time he passed it, he couldn't dare risk entering it again. Not now, not when Tryggr would instantly scent it upon him.

And Tryggr did scent for it, Eben was almost certain. Every day when Eben stepped into the scullery, Tryggr's frowning eyes would dart up, his nostrils flaring. And Eben couldn't deny scenting Tryggr, too, seeking out any changes, any new traces of other orcs—but there was still nothing. Still only *him.*

It made it too easy to beam at Tryggr's watching, wary eyes, and then even to shyly greet the scullery's other occupants. This almost always included Duff, but often an eager young Grisk named Timo, an indolent Bautul named Gaukr, and the Ash-Kai cook Gegnir—and, of course, Alma herself. And Eben had been pleased to see that Alma's condition had continued to steadily improve, to the point where she'd not only taken over the management of the scullery, but also the mountain's overall housekeeping efforts—essentially fulfilling the empty role of the mountain's former Keeper. A considerable and often thankless endeavour, to be sure, but Alma embraced the work with genuine-seeming enthusiasm, and treated her helpers with quiet, consistent kindness.

"Thank you so much," she would say to Eben, warm and earnest, whenever he brought in some lye, or drain cleaner, or even a long brush to scrub out the vents. "That will be a great help, I'm sure."

Eben always flushed and waved it away, though he often found himself glancing toward her afterwards, inhaling slow and deep. Not only scenting for any signs of further weakness or illness upon her, but also breathing in the distinct scents of Drafli and Baldr, now woven into her own, and deepening with every passing day. Suggesting, much to Eben's ongoing surprise and relief, that Drafli had indeed continued to honour the terms of that astonishing offer he'd made, welcoming Alma into his relationship, and his bed. Drafli had even made Alma kneel and suck his seed in the scullery, clearly marking both her and the room with his scent, as a true orc mate would—and according to Tryggr's gleeful retelling, Drafli had even done it while Tryggr and Duff had watched, signing her cool, casual orders that she'd instantly and eagerly obeyed.

Tryggr's admiring envy as he'd recounted the tale had been blatantly clear, prompting Eben to pay far closer attention to the Skai sign language, while also keeping an admittedly too-curious eye out for any sign of Drafli's return. And though he was disappointed in that regard, Eben also hadn't missed how several new buckets and cleaning implements had mysteriously appeared, bearing only Drafli's scent—and after hearing about the rodent infestation from Tryggr, Drafli had apparently even gone and brought Alma a *cat*.

If she can keep it up, show Boss she's worth his time, I ken he'll come around...

It was more relief in Eben's thoughts, more hope curling low in his belly. And as the days passed, it made it easier to laugh and chat—and even sign—with his new colleagues, and to keep offering whatever help he could. Which had so far included a thorough cleaning of the drain and vents, an expansion and repair of the ash chute, an ongoing supply of lye and chalk for soap and stains, and help with folding and delivering the laundry when needed. Eben had even begun a daily delivery of fresh tonic for Duff, formulated to include several of the proteins present in rat-meat. Which proved such a success that Tryggr showed up early one morning in the sickroom, and flashed Eben a sheepish smile from across the workbench.

"Duff's not feeling so good today," Tryggr said, "and he's been asking for the sweet Ka-esh's sweet drink. Would you mind making a batch early?"

Eben didn't mind at all, of course, and instantly set to work mixing it up, while Tryggr watched over the workbench. And though Eben's hands still shook as he worked, he managed not to spill anything, and smiled at Tryggr as he gave the bottle one final shake, and passed it over to him.

"I hope this helps," he said shyly. "I am glad he likes it."

Tryggr twitched a nod, his eyes lingering oddly on Eben's face. "Ach, he does," he replied. "An' I ken it does help him— he's always a bit more easy and alert afterwards. Enough to even keep making a fool of himself over that lazy arse Gaukr."

Eben couldn't help a laugh—Duff and Gaukr had begun a halting romance of sorts, these past days—but then he found that Tryggr was still hesitating, studying him over the workbench. His mouth pursed, his head tilted, his brow slowly furrowing.

"So... where'd you learn it all, anyway, Ka-esh?" he asked, his voice carefully light. "All this"—he gestured vaguely around at the sickroom—"and everything you know about the scullery, too? The vents, the drains, the chutes? The chalk for the bloodstains? How to make lye?"

More heat pooled into Eben's face, but he shrugged and gave a dismissive wave of his hand. "Most of it from reading and studying, I ken," he said, as steadily as he could. "The lye and chalk have oft been discussed in medical journals and treatises, for keeping clean is of great import in healing wounds, ach? And the engineering, I trained for many, many years upon this, for I was meant to be—"

His voice tripped, caught in his throat, but before him, Tryggr was still waiting, listening, his eyes curious and intent. So Eben forced himself to swallow, to draw in a deep breath of Tryggr's sweet scent. Still with only him, only him, upon it.

"I was meant to be our clan's Chief Structural Engineer," he said thickly. "Just as my father, and his father before him. But I wished—to learn medicine, instead. To seek answers to what ails our kin and our women, and offer the help they need."

Tryggr's eyes shifted, his head tilting a little further. "You have regrets, though?" he asked, careful now. "Wish you'd gone for the fancy title after all? Probably came with plenty of credits and acclaim, I ken?"

His voice sounded skeptical, almost suspicious, and curse it, Eben's scent must have betrayed something, must have hinted at all that old whispering darkness. And he had to draw in another deep, dragging breath, hold it in, only him, only him...

"I only regret—my father," he croaked out, his lip quivering hard enough that he bit down painfully against it. "He never forgave me for abandoning his great work, and he banished me from—our lives. Our home. Even upon his deathbed, he did not—"

He couldn't finish it, squeezing his eyes shut, shaking his head. And for an instant, there was silence before him, heavy and watchful—and then the feel of a warm, strong hand, gripping at his shoulder.

"Real sorry to hear that, Ka-esh," came Tryggr's low voice. "Your pa was a fool for not seeing how good you are at your work. An' how important it is, too."

Eben's shocked eyes blinked open, searching Tryggr's face,

but there was no mockery in it, no trace of guile or sarcasm. Only a strange, serious stillness, something almost like... respect.

"It's good work, Ka-esh," Tryggr said, with a gentle squeeze to Eben's arm. "Real good, ach?"

What? Tryggr didn't... mean that. Did he? He thought Eben's work was good? Truly?

But yes, Tryggr was still looking at him like that, still holding Eben's shoulder, and now twitching a sad little smile. "You deserved better, Ka-esh," he said. "Not sure how I got two good fathers—between Pa and *Pabbi*—and you got dumped with yours. Don't seem fair, does it?"

Eben swallowed, his scrambling thoughts fighting to follow, to focus. Because yes, Tryggr had mentioned his father before, hadn't he? But he'd never brought up his *pabbi*—his adopted father—right?

"What—what are your fathers like?" Eben managed. "Are they both—good to you? Do they uphold—your goals? Your work?"

Tryggr's mouth twitched, his eyes flickering with warm, wry fondness. "Ach, always," he said. "Though it oft takes a bit of fussing to sort out, you ken. Pa first got it into his thick head that I oughta be a great Skai warrior, leading battles and such—but once I told him I'd rather work for Boss, he blustered for a day or two, and then went and set it all up for me. Told Boss he'd be a fool not to take me."

A small smile pulled at Eben's mouth—Tryggr's pa had to be a fearsome orc, to make demands of Drafli like that—and Tryggr's smile widened too, as he huffed a rueful little chuckle. "Don't mean Pa don't still try to poke his nose in wherever he can, though," he added lightly, with a roll of his eyes. "Thank Skai-kesh, *Pabbi* usually settles him down, and keeps him in line. Without him, I ken Pa would be sniffing about the scullery every damned day, asking after the sweet Ka-esh's scent. *Again.*"

Wait. Tryggr meant—his pa had been asking about... Eben? About Eben's scent? About Eben's scent on *Tryggr*, he surely meant, because of course Tryggr's family would smell it, and wonder at it. Wouldn't they?

And curse it, Eben's breath was coming too hard, the longing shivering fast and hungry into his scent. Strong enough that perhaps Tryggr had caught it too, his eyes gone blank as he twitched backwards, away—but then he hesitated, and raised the jar of milk toward Eben, as if in a little salute.

"Well, thanks again, Ka-esh," he said, husky. "An' see you later today?"

Eben fervently nodded and smiled, and again made the Skai sign for *thank you*, his hand over his heart. A movement that Tryggr looked at for an instant too long before he turned toward the door—but just before he left, he hesitated, and made a sign back, too. *My honour*, it said.

Eben couldn't stop smiling to himself for the rest of the day, as the happiness kept circling and skittering in his chest. Tryggr had come to see him. Tryggr had wanted his tonic. Tryggr had told him about his family. And most powerful of all, Tryggr had praised Eben's work.

Your pa was a fool. It's good work. Real good.

It was something no one else had ever said to Eben, not that he could ever recall. Among the Ka-esh, an engineer remained the highest possible calling, commanding praise and respect, while medicine was new, untested, unfamiliar. Something done mostly by the Ash-Kai clan, with their gifted healers like Eftcrar—or perhaps sometimes by the Grisk, with their care for kin and home. Until Eben, and then Salvi after him, it had never been a Ka-esh discipline, not in the slightest. And to be told—by a Skai!—of its worth felt deeply, fundamentally powerful. Like something Eben would forever treasure, for all his days.

That afternoon in the scullery, it was even easier to chat

and laugh with Tryggr and Duff—who'd eagerly drunk the second bottle of tonic Eben had brought him—and with Alma, too. Alma still wasn't in the scullery as often as Tryggr and Duff, due to her ever-expanding work as the mountain's new Keeper, but today she was making more soap, while excitedly reviewing their plans to do a full floor-washing, all throughout the mountain.

It was an endeavour that required flooding the mountain from the top, and it had needed considerable amounts of Ka-esh input, including the involvement of multiple engineers. And Eben had willingly taken the lead on the Ka-esh side of the project, collecting and combining all the engineers' notes, reviewing and translating them into common-tongue, and adding his own annotations. And just the evening before, he'd finished a comprehensive summary of required processes and estimated timelines for Alma, so she could assign tasks to her helpers as needed, and create a proper schedule for the day.

"That document has just been so helpful," she said warmly over her shoulder, toward where Eben was currently hanging the clean wet laundry on the wall's rickety drying racks. "Thank you so much for pulling it together on such short notice. It must have been a shocking amount of work, on top of all your work in the sickroom."

Eben shrugged and waved it away, though he couldn't quite suppress his small, grateful smile toward her. To which Alma smiled back, a flush spreading across her pretty face—even as a dark, bitter scent filtered from Tryggr at the washbasin.

"So how're things going with Boss these days, woman?" Tryggr cut in, his voice sharp. "He still treating you properly, training you up, showing you off? Giving you lots of joy with his mate?"

Alma's face flushed even redder, and she mumbled something unintelligible toward the sink. But there was no mistaking the sudden surge of hunger and longing and pleasure in her scent, so strong it nearly swayed Eben on his feet, and flared a stab of envy deep into his belly. What must it be like, to have such a fearsome Skai treating you properly, training you up, showing you off? Giving you joy?

He'll come around, Tryggr had said. *If she can keep it up, show she's worth his time...*

Eben couldn't help a furtive look toward Tryggr at the basin, and found him frowning down at the water, his brow deeply furrowed. Looking so strangely troubled that Eben felt his own happiness—his own hopefulness—slightly faltering, skittering into his fingers. Into where he foolishly fumbled at a bar of the drying rack, and knocked half of it out of the damned wall entirely.

"Ach, Ka-esh!" Tryggr snapped, as he lurched over, and caught the bars before they tumbled to the floor. "Watch yourself!"

Oh. A cold shudder rippled up Eben's spine, his head instantly ducking, his eyes squeezing shut. "Sorry, sir," he croaked, thick in his throat. "It was a—a—"

An accident, he'd meant to say, but oh, he couldn't even speak, the sudden misery churning in his belly, flooding hot into his chest. Foolish. *Foolish*. And Tryggr was still frowning at him like that, like he was foolish, weak—and curse it, Eben wasn't about to start weeping, not here, not now, not where they all could see—

He mumbled a choked, halting excuse, and then spun around, and dodged for the door. Rushing out through the kitchen, into the corridor, as the vision of the distant Ka-esh wing bloomed behind his eyes. The vision of the *dýflissa*, yes, with its sweet promises of relief, of pain, of forgetting. It had been so long, the longest Eben could remember going without being touched in his entire adult life, and he just needed—he needed—

He crashed. Smashing straight into something warm and

solid, sending him reeling backwards, staggering on his feet. Blinking, focusing, as more miserable panic shot through his chest, through his trembling, gulping mouth...

It was Drafli.

15

Drafli. The most terrifying orc in the mountain, *here*, looming over Eben in the dark empty corridor, and glowering at him with narrow, furious-looking eyes.

Fuck, how the hell did Eben keep doing this. Foolish, *foolish*, and visions of Drafli's dagger were already whirling into his thoughts, screaming behind his eyes. *Never let a Skai get you alone, run, run, run—*

But then Drafli—signed at him. Spoke to him, with the Skai sign language, slow and distinct enough that Eben could easily follow what it meant.

Wait, he signed. *Peace. Tryggr will come.*

What? No. No, he wouldn't, he wasn't, foolish, and Eben's darting glance up the corridor found only blackness, and more desperate panic in his chest. He was alone with Drafli. Drafli who had almost murdered Alma, and who now... scented of Alma. Scented of Alma, on his hands, his groin, his mouth, his... breath. And suddenly there was the jolting, utterly incongruous vision of Drafli with his face buried between Alma's legs, his cruel tongue licking her from the inside out, and he—he hadn't. Had he?

But it was still there on Drafli's scent, bright and clear, just as vivid as if Eben had seen it with his own eyes. And now that Eben was studying Drafli, breathing him in this close, he still scented only of Alma and Baldr, too. Shouting that he'd still kept those vows. Kept to the terms of that offer he'd made. *Never trust a Skai...*

And wait, now Drafli was glancing purposefully up the corridor—and yes, oh, he'd somehow spoken truth in that, too. Because Tryggr was indeed jogging down the corridor toward them, his mouth grim, his eyes darting rapid and unreadable between Drafli and Eben.

Good, Drafli signed sharply at Tryggr, while running his piercing gaze up and down Eben's still-shivering body. *Now tend to him. You cannot allow your——to scent thus.*

Eben's blinking eyes hadn't at all caught what Drafli had called him, but Tryggr clearly understood, giving a shaky exhale, and a jerky nod. To which Drafli nodded too, and made to turn away—but then he stopped, and spun back to Tryggr again. *He is——*, he signed. *He helped me in a time of——, and spared me from a——wrong.*

Oh. Eben's racing heart skipped a beat, his eyes now darting between Drafli's hands and his face. Because Drafli hadn't just said that—whatever the full extent of it was—about him? But yes, yes, Drafli had given a curt nod between him and Tryggr, and then strode off up the corridor, not sparing a single look back.

It left Eben standing there blinking uneasily at Tryggr, who still looked distinctly uneasy, too. His face pale, his shoulders heaving, his swallow convulsing in his corded throat.

"Ach, Ka-esh," he said thickly. "You're all right, ach? No need to scent thus. Naught to fear."

Right. Eben couldn't hide his grimace, his eyes dropping, because of course Tryggr would only think he was afraid, and in need of comforting. Foolish, weak...

"An'—I'm sorry," Tryggr continued, faster. "Didn't mean to snap at you, or run you off like that, just now. I wasn't vexed with you, or tryna mock or shame you, ach? Could never be vexed with you, you ken. Was just"—he drew in a deep breath—"fussing over you, is all. Just means—I care."

Oh. *Oh.* Something warm and trembly shivered up Eben's spine, and his eyes snapped up, searching Tryggr's pale, watching face. He... meant that? He... cared?

"Oh," Eben whispered, without at all meaning to. "I—thank you, sir."

Tryggr's eyes briefly closed, his head tilting back in a way that looked almost despairing. "Ach, Ka-esh," he said, hoarse. "Don't need to thank me, either."

But Eben was searching him now, drinking in that undeniable truth of his own scent, and only his scent, on Tryggr's twitching, too-close body. Just like Drafli had only borne Baldr and Alma's scents... the same Drafli who had kept his word, and even praised Eben's efforts. His help.

Eben gathered his breath, gathered his courage, as his own trembling, tingling hand moved. Slipping up between them, slow, shaky—and then very lightly, very carefully, stroking up against Tryggr's warm bare chest.

"But you have been—so kind, sir," he ventured, very quiet. "It—pleases me, to thank you. To—honour you."

And oh, oh, what had he just said, what the hell was he doing—and he snatched his hand away, too late. But it still felt hot, trembly, alive with the feel of Tryggr's smooth warm skin, with the truth of his rich scent now lingering on Eben's fingers. And Tryggr's scent in the air had shifted too, flaring with something bright and sweet...

But Tryggr hadn't moved, or made any indication of responding in turn, and his face still looked pale, his jaw flexing in his cheek. "Ach, Ka-esh," he finally said. "Then— next time I speak thus to you, mayhap you'll just—ignore me.

Or throw it back at me. But there's no need to run away, or scent as though I've just gone and kicked you in the heart, ach? 'Cause I'd *never*."

Oh. Well. Eben's relief exhaled heavy and harsh, and he could feel the slow smile pulling at his mouth, warming his eyes. "I am... glad," he murmured. "I... thank you, sir."

Tryggr half-laughed, half-groaned, his eyes glinting on Eben's face with frustration, and exasperation, and... something else. And for a breathless, dangling instant, Eben thought he might come closer, might even reach out and...

But then Tryggr cleared his throat, and took a purposeful step backwards. "You oughta get to bed, then, Ka-esh," he said firmly. "Big day tomorrow, ach?"

Right. Eben had of course committed to a full day of work supporting Alma's floor-cleaning project, and he jerked a nod, and fought to ignore the sharp little plunge in his belly. To which Tryggr let out another low, frustrated-sounding groan, as he lurched forward—and before Eben had even caught it, Tryggr bent over him, and pressed a soft, brief kiss to the top of his head.

"Sleep well, sweet Ka-esh," he said gruffly, as he backed away again, not meeting Eben's eyes. "See you tomorrow."

Eben couldn't even nod, let alone speak, and he stood frozen in place, tingling all over, watching Tryggr stride away up the corridor. His steps long and quick, his shoulders square, his hand rubbing at his face as he disappeared around the corner.

Tryggr had... kissed him. He'd *kissed* him.

It was a bright, jubilant awareness, firing warm and hopeful through Eben's chest. *Keep it up. Show him. He'll come around...*

Eben slept deep and contented that night, and the next morning he first stopped by the sickroom, checking with Efterar and preparing any urgent prescriptions, before heading to the scullery. Where he again threw himself into another full, intensive day of work, not only supporting Alma's project as best as he could, but dealing with the Ka-esh engineers—who made it clear they would rather be doing anything else—while also personally ensuring the sickroom got the deepest, most thorough cleaning possible. To the point where, late in the day, even Kesst looked satisfied, smiling gratefully at Eben as a faintly snoring Efterar slept soundly in a nearby bed.

"Looks and scents so much better, doesn't it?" Kesst said, without even a trace of mockery or sarcasm in his voice. "Such a damned relief. It was good of you Ka-esh to help Alma organize it all."

Eben smiled and waved it away—or at least, he attempted to, because suddenly a familiar scent had swarmed into the room, and snatched at his hand in midair. And even as Eben startled to look, he already knew—it was Tryggr. Tryggr, here, gripping his hand, and flashing Kesst a broad, if rather chilly, smile.

"It was good of *this* Ka-esh, you mean," he said to Kesst, as his hand gently squeezed Eben's. "You ken the rest of 'em woulda done near as much without him? He don't oft draw eyes to himself, but he's been working his pretty little arse off on this. Just like he does every day in here, too—not that any of *you* can be fussed to notice."

Eben froze to stunned stillness, his eyes aghast on Tryggr's face. He hadn't just said that... had he? To *Kesst*? One of the most popular, influential orcs in the mountain?!

But to Eben's ongoing astonishment, Kesst blinked between them, and then grimaced, and let out a heavy sigh. "Right," he said. "Sorry. I suppose it's—easy to overlook individual contributions in here, amidst all the filth and blood and exhaustion."

With that, he gave a wild-looking wave that seemed to encompass the entire room, before spinning and stalking off again. But beside Eben, Tryggr looked at least somewhat mollified, and more warmth was pooling and fizzing in Eben's belly.

Tryggr had defended him. Tryggr had noticed his work. Tryggr had noticed his *pretty little arse*.

"Now c'mon, Ka-esh," Tryggr said firmly, with a gentle tug at where he was still holding Eben's hand. "You *reek* of weariness, and you're going to bed, ach?"

Eben meekly nodded, and willingly allowed Tryggr to lead him out the door, and down toward the Ka-esh wing. But instead of stopping and sending Eben onward, as Eben fully expected, Tryggr kept walking beside him, his grip on Eben's hand warm and firm, his eyes frowning on the corridor up ahead.

"It *was* real good of you, to do all that work today," Tryggr finally said, into the silence. "Heard you going at it with some of those Ka-esh earlier, spurring 'em on. I ken they'd have all stayed hunkered down here buried in their rocks and books, without you."

He wasn't wrong, and Eben huffed a short, wry little laugh. "Ach, well, we are not always naturally inclined to see beyond our own clan, I ken," he said. "Or beyond our books, either."

They'd reached the door of his room, and Eben shot a rueful glance at his own refreshed pile of books, stacked high on his small, rickety desk. With his enforced early bedtimes, he'd continued to expand his reading, and he was vaguely surprised to see Tryggr's mouth drop open, his eyes incredulous on Eben's face.

"Wait, Ka-esh," he snapped. "When I've been sending you to bed, you've been coming down here alone into this dank little hole, and *reading*, instead of sleeping?"

Eben blinked and bit his lip, the chagrin curdling sudden and sharp through his chest. "Um, I—" he began, between shaky breaths. "Just—a little? I just—*need* to read, sir."

He was cringing away, his eyes wide and fearful on Tryggr's face—but wait. Something was hitching in Tryggr's scent, something that called up a dark, ravenous hunger low in Eben's belly—and oh, Tryggr's hand was clasping tighter on Eben's, drawing him closer, as his other hand reached around, and gave a gentle slap to Eben's *arse.*

"I oughta thrash you for this, little Ka-esh," Tryggr breathed. "Oughta bend you over my knee, and teach you a fucking *lesson.*"

Oh, *fuck.* Eben's gasp was almost a groan, dragging low and hungry out of his throat, shuddering his body all over, leaning closer into Tryggr's touch. Because oh, please, yes, would Tryggr really do that, please, *now—*

But curse him, maybe he'd betrayed too much, because Tryggr abruptly lurched backwards, rubbing his hand forcefully at his eyes. "Just joking!" he said, his voice far louder than before. "Just want you to sleep, Ka-esh! That's *all.*"

He didn't wait for Eben's reply, and instead whirled around, and fled from the room. Leaving Eben standing there and breathing hard, his face hot, his cock rigid and straining helplessly in his trousers. What... what had that been about? Had Eben... truly displeased Tryggr, with the books? Upset him? Or was this just... not working, after all? Did Tryggr just... not care? Even with the truth of only Eben's scent upon him?

Never trust a Skai, his father's voice droned, and Eben squeezed his eyes shut, and shook his head. *Show him. He'll come around. I oughta bend you over my knee...*

Sleep was slow coming that night, amidst all the doubts and thwarted hunger now swirling Eben's thoughts, and he slept in far too late the next morning—but he gathered his determination as he washed and dressed, fetched a bucket of lye, and headed back up into the mountain. He had to keep trying. Tryggr would come around...

His heart pounded louder as he neared the scullery, his breaths short and shallow in his throat—but yes, yes, he could scent Tryggr, could see him just ahead, there. Alone in the scullery, bent over the washbasin, scrubbing at a stained tunic.

But for perhaps the first time since they'd begun this, Tryggr didn't acknowledge Eben's approach. Didn't even look up. Just kept frowning down at his scrubbing, his mouth set and thin, his scent strange in the air.

"Is aught—amiss, sir?" Eben asked, before he could help it. "Are you—feeling well?"

Tryggr huffed a laugh and shook his head, but kept his eyes on his scrubbing. "Ach, well enough," he said, aiming a brief glower over his shoulder toward the still-looming pile of laundry on the counter. "Just—weary of laundry, mayhap."

Of course. Tryggr had been washing clothes for multiple days on end now, and Eben felt a sudden jolt of sympathy, and perhaps regret, too. Despite all his efforts here, he'd so rarely thought about seeking ways to specifically help Tryggr—he always seemed so capable, so relaxed, so self-assured. But now, blinking at Tryggr's bowed head, it occurred to Eben that he did look weary, and a little sad, too. And for a Skai who was trained as a scout and a warrior, being ordered onto laundry duty for so long must have been a miserable—or even humiliating—experience, right? And how had Eben never considered that, never once considered how Tryggr might feel about all this?

"Well, I have been thinking," Eben said, too quickly, "that we ought to seek ways to make this washing more efficient. I have been meaning to speak to our engineers upon this, for I have read of machines in the north that can help, and make this faster."

His voice came out too eager, almost desperate, but Tryggr still didn't spare a look up. "Ach, mayhap," he said distractedly. "Thanks, Ka-esh."

Eben's belly dipped, his throat swallowing hard, but he jerked a nod, and made to stagger with the increasingly heavy bucket of lye toward the sink—a movement that finally snapped Tryggr's head up, his eyes flashing with sudden disbelief.

"Ach, Ka-esh!" he yelped, as he leapt to his feet. "Careful! Give me that!"

Right. Eben's belly plummeted again, but he managed another nod, and shoved the bucket toward Tryggr's waiting hands. And then attempted a smile up toward his face, as Tryggr's words from the corridor echoed through his thoughts. *Just fussing over you. Just means—I care.*

And surely Tryggr was thinking of it too, his eyes oddly intent on Eben's face as he took the bucket, their fingers just brushing— but then Tryggr's gaze shifted purposefully beyond Eben. Toward where—oh. Alma. Scenting of uncertainty, and looking mean- ingfully toward Tryggr, as though she wished to speak with him.

Eben could take a hint, at least, so he rushed out the door, and headed back to the sickroom. Where he barely noticed Kesst's nod toward him as he entered—at least, until Kesst sighed, and came over to eye Eben over the workbench.

"Look, I just wanted to—apologize, again, for overlooking all your efforts, Eben," he said. "And for pushing you to help in the scullery, and teasing you like I did about Alma, too. I know it's not an excuse, but I've been a bit—out of sorts, lately."

Eben blinked, genuinely taken aback, but he attempted to smile, and wave it away. But perhaps it hadn't come out right, because Kesst sighed again, and gave Eben a look that was almost... sympathetic. "And I didn't even notice," he added, quieter, "that it's not Alma you've been pining over all this time, is it? It's that loudmouth Skai fuckboy *Tryggr*. Gods, you two even *scent* of each other."

Wait. No. Damn it. Eben couldn't move, couldn't breathe, could only stare aghast at Kesst's face, because now Kesst would tell Tryggr how Eben felt, Kesst would mock him and dismiss him and ruin everything—

"Gods, don't scent like that, I won't *tell* him," Kesst said, flapping a hand toward him. "I just thought maybe I owed you—a warning."

A warning. Eben still couldn't breathe, could only stand there and wait while his stomach pitched and churned in his gut, and Kesst sighed again. "You just—you know what Skai can be like, right?" he said thinly. "I mean, I know they're not all like that, I'm trying to examine my own biases here, but still, just"—he hesitated, his eyes almost sad on Eben's face—"just... be careful. You could end up—really hurt."

Oh. Eben's heart was erratically pinging in his chest, but he made himself nod, and mumble a thank-you. And long after Kesst had gone back to his own work, his words kept echoing through Eben's thoughts, again and again and again. *You know what Skai are like. Be careful. You could end up really hurt. Never trust a Skai...*

By the end of the workday, Eben was sweaty and jittery and half-panicked, rushing back to the scullery with shaky, frantic steps. But his heart dropped even before he entered, because he could already scent that Tryggr wasn't there—or Alma, either. Only Duff was still working, doggedly sloshing soapy water against a bloodstained pair of trousers.

"Young Tryg not here," he balefully informed Eben, without being asked. "In Skai arena, I ken."

Eben fought to quash his surging disappointment, and attempted to focus on helping with some washing instead. But Duff kept darting narrow glances toward him, and finally he bobbed his silver head toward the door. "You go," he said. "Fetch him yourself."

What? No. Eben couldn't possibly go to that terrifying arena, not alone, not again—but Duff jabbed a soapy, wizened finger at the door this time. "No Skai dare touch you," he said flatly, "now you bear young Tryg scent."

Oh. Truly? And Eben hadn't at all realized Duff knew about

that, but of course he would have scented it, just like Kesst, just like Tryggr's fathers, just like they all had, perhaps. And it was enough to make Eben nod, to make him lurch for the door again. Not thinking, not thinking, as he staggered on shaky legs toward the Skai wing, his heartbeat thundering distantly through his chest. He was just walking, just seeking that sweet familiar scent, that was all, that was all...

And yes, yes, there it was, just a twinge of it, drawing Eben down this corridor, down that one. Winding deeper and deeper into the dim cozy Skai wing, and between the scent and the comforting darkness, it kept his steps moving, going, closer and closer and closer...

Until—this. This door. The arena. With far fewer scents flooding it this time, and Eben's eyes instantly caught on Tryggr. He was fighting against three other Skai orcs, his lean body writhing and snapping and kicking, his grunts and hisses filtering through the air. And for a startled, frozen instant, Eben could only stand there and stare at him, drink up the fierce fluid beauty of his strong, stunning body. Damn, he was gorgeous, he was everything, and there was nothing more Eben wanted than to...

But then, Tryggr froze. His head snapping up, his gaze darting toward—Eben. And for an instant, they only stared at each other, even as another orc landed what looked like a painful kick into Tryggr's side, setting him staggering on his feet, pitching sideways, toward...

Eben. Wait, wait, Tryggr was coming toward Eben, sprinting with astonishing speed, his eyes blazing. And before Eben could move, or catch it, or speak, Tryggr dragged him out into the corridor, shoved him up against the hard stone wall, and   pinned him there. Trapped him there.

Oh, this wasn't happening, it couldn't be happening—but it was, Tryggr's lean sweaty body was hot and shivery and far too close, his scent flooding all through Eben's breath. And oh, oh, his face was even nuzzling into Eben's neck, and inhaling slow and deep, while his hungry clawed hand slipped up Eben's chest, too. Moving slowly enough that Eben could easily knock it away, could run or refuse or escape—but instead he moaned and shivered all over as that hand found his neck, and circled certain and safe around it.

Fuck. Fuck, yes, this was what he wanted, what he needed, what he'd been craving all this time, and he arched up into it, offering his neck, offering anything Tryggr would take, anything he would give. And Tryggr would, he *was*, his teeth scraping against Eben's collarbone, seeking the best place to bite and drink, please, please...

But then—it was gone. Gone, gone, because Tryggr was staggering backwards, whipping his head back and forth, dragging his hands against his hair. And Eben was already following, desperate and instinctive, his hand reaching out, just needing it back, please, please—

"No, Ka-esh," Tryggr hissed, sharp and low, almost a bark. "I said, no!"

It was as though he'd struck Eben across the face, and Eben froze, stunned, mortified, as ice kicked and cracked in his belly. No? No?

"Look, I just—I can't, Ka-esh," Tryggr said, and he'd even spun away from Eben, his head tilting back, his hands rubbing at his face. "I know what you really want, and I just—can't, all right? I've seen it with Pa an' *Pabbi*, my whole fucking life, and I'm not gonna—ach. No. *No*."

No. Eben couldn't breathe, couldn't think, could scarcely even follow Tryggr's words. He couldn't. He couldn't. He was saying no, no, *no*.

No.

"Look, I'm sorry," Tryggr said, too thick, still without looking at Eben. "But I just—just need some time away from you for a spell, ach? Naught personal, it's not your fault, but you're just too—you just make me—I just—I *can't*, Ka-esh."

Oh. And even if Eben still couldn't follow the rest of it, he could follow this. Tryggr didn't want him. Tryggr wanted him to go away. After all that, after all Eben's foolish hopes and plans and longings, Tryggr was saying—no.

And it was as though something had broken, wretched and raw, deep in Eben's chest, in his heart. Something deeper than loss, or despair, so deep Eben couldn't bear to touch it, to look at it. Couldn't bear to even look at Tryggr, couldn't bear to scent him for another breath.

"Ach, then," he whispered, to the floor, go, go, go. "You shall not see me again."

And before he could buckle beneath it, he spun around, and staggered into the darkness.

16

Eben didn't know how he ended up in the Ka-esh wing, staring at the *dýflissa*.

The scents of pain and pleasure were so familiar, so sweet, the sounds of firm slaps and cracking whips thudding deep into his aching chest. But his prick stayed soft and slack in his trousers, and a distant part of Eben pointed out that he was so often soft, in the *dýflissa*. It wasn't like those moments with Tryggr, with all that desire and longing. It was... empty. Just as empty as he was.

"Eben?" asked a voice, Gareth's voice, and Eben blinked at where his familiar form was striding out of the *dýflissa*, his whip still in hand, his trousers sagging around his sweaty waist. "What is amiss? Are you hurt?"

Eben couldn't even speak, could only stare blankly at Gareth's face, at the slowly increasing concern in his eyes. "Is it that Skai?" Gareth demanded, sharper now. "What has he done to you?"

But it was enough to rouse some faint awareness in Eben's chest, and he shook his head. "He did naught," he said dully. "Naught at all."

Gareth kept studying him, the worry creasing his forehead. "Should you mayhap... wish for some relief, then?" he asked, tentative. "I should be glad to offer whatever you wish."

He'd even held up the whip, but still nothing stirred in Eben's trousers, and now he could hear Tryggr's voice again, echoing behind his blinking eyes. *Not much relief if it brings you real harm, is it? Keeps you running back for more?*

Eben's head seemed to shake on its own, and his sad little smile almost felt genuine. "Thank you, brother," he whispered, "but I ken it should be wiser to rest."

He was vaguely surprised at the strength of the disappointment in Gareth's scent, but he suddenly felt too weary to wonder at it. Too weary even to return to his own room, on the opposite side of the Ka-esh wing—and instead, his numb, staggering feet took him to a different room. A far larger room, just a corridor over, reeking of familiarity and pain.

His family's room. Their *hellir*.

Eben hadn't stepped foot in it since his father's death years before, but he was unsurprised to see that it hadn't been changed, or put to another use. It would still be considered his own *hellir* by the clan, even after all this time, and the furnishings were all still here, even his father's old clothes, now surely ruined by moths and mildew. And Eben blinked around at it for a dazed, stilted moment, before lurching over to sink onto his old stone bunk, burying his face in his hands.

Never trust a Skai, his father's voice shouted, so loud now. *You never focus on what is important. You waste your talent and your time. You do a deep disservice to all your Ka-esh kin. You show yourself foolish and weak.*

Get out. Do not return here or speak to me again, until you come to your senses.

Eben's mouth choked a sound like a laugh, or a sob, because he had never come to his senses, had he? He'd always been a disappointment, a failure, a waste for his kin and his clan. He'd always known it, his father had always known it, *never trust a Skai...*

Another sob tore from Eben's chest, heaving out of his trembling mouth. *Never trust a Skai.* A refrain, a mantra, a curse, that had spoken so strongly of his father's conviction, his clan's truth. And Eben had believed it, had believed it and feared it, just as he'd believed and feared all the rest of it, and maybe—

His head shook in his hands as more thick, ugly sobs barked from his throat. He'd believed it all for so, so long. And maybe—maybe Tryggr had been—a hint of light, in the darkness. A rebellion. *I can show you the way.*

Because with Tryggr, Eben had fought against his father's words, even as he'd still feared them. For if a Skai could be trusted, after all, then maybe—maybe the rest of it might have been wrong, too.

You never focus on what is important. You waste your talent and your time. You show yourself foolish and weak...

But Tryggr—Tryggr had never treated Eben that way, not once. He'd never thought him or his efforts a waste. Even tonight, even amidst all that hurt and grief, Tryggr hadn't been harsh or cruel. *I'm sorry. Naught personal. Not your fault.*

The sobs kept choking from Eben's throat, his head shaking against his trembling fingers, but Tryggr's voice kept speaking now, steady and certain and so, so confident. *No need to apologize. Don't speak thus. I've got you. Naught to fear.*

It was good of you, Ka-esh. Brave as hell. You didn't need to do it, and you did it anyway. We're grateful.

And even stronger, sharper, those heady, impossible moments in Eben's room, with his head in Tryggr's lap. *Good. Real good, Ka-esh. Ach, you've got a tight, hot little mouth. Real nice. So good and tight and sweet, so pretty with a Skai in your mouth...*

But beyond that, even strongest of all, was still that day in the sickroom, when Tryggr had come to ask for Eben's tonic.

For Eben's work. When he'd looked Eben in the eye, and spoken those impossible, unthinkable words, words Eben would never forget.

It's good work, Ka-esh. Real good. Your pa was a fool for not seeing how good you are at your work. An' how important it is, too.

Your pa was a fool. It's good work. Real good.

The words rang around and around in Eben's skull, behind his scratchy eyes, curling into his empty-feeling chest. *It's good work. Real good.*

And amidst his hollow, aching exhaustion, Eben could somehow, almost... agree. It *was* good work. It was. He'd seen how it had helped Duff. He'd seen how it had helped countless other patients, orcs, women, orclings. And that truth—that help—wasn't something his father could ever take from him.

His father had been... wrong.

Never trust a Skai, the grating voice chanted, but Eben shook his head, and drew in a deep, dragging breath. Because maybe... maybe his father had been wrong about that too, after all. Even if Tryggr hadn't wanted Eben, or hadn't even liked him—he'd still been so kind. So consistently generous. He'd looked out for Eben, he'd helped him, he'd praised him.

If nothing else, Tryggr had been... a friend. A real friend, who could be trusted, and relied upon.

And that, too, was something else Eben was sure about. Even if his own perceptions couldn't be trusted, Tryggr had still been a true friend to Alma. To Duff. Even to Drafli, doing all that miserable work in the scullery, seeking to support his boss in a time of great personal difficulty, and helping to make his new woman feel at home.

And yes, even Drafli had trusted Tryggr. The fiercest, most fearsome Skai in the mountain had trusted Tryggr alone with his woman, for days and days on end. And Tryggr had returned that trust with hard work, and with care, and with kindness.

Never trust a... began the voice, but Eben shook his head, and curled up on the bunk.

Your pa was a fool. It's good work. Real good.

He somehow slept like that, alone on the hard cold stone, breathing the scents of his father, his lost home. He even dreamt of his father, of his father speaking, speaking, speaking, hurling his conviction and his fear at his small, cowering child. A child who finally raised his wet, miserable face, and whispered, *It is good work, Father. It is.*

When Eben awoke again, his head still ached, his eyes puffy and gritty, his throat still raw from his weeping. But the emptiness in his chest had shifted, somehow, settled into a strange, unfamiliar certainty.

It was good work. It had been a good choice. He had worked hard, and done his best.

But then—he blinked, rubbed his face—a scent. A familiar scent. A scent he'd never expected to taste this close again, still whispering of... him.

"Tryggr?" he croaked, toward the door—and in a flash of movement, Tryggr indeed lurched into view. Hovering in the doorway with an odd, jerky intensity, his forehead furrowed, his face pale.

"Sorry to bother you, Ka-esh," he said, his voice rough. "But there's been a bit of a mess up above, and I was wondering if you might be willing to—"

He broke off there, wincing, but Eben was already shoving himself up in bed, and nodding. Tryggr had been a friend. A gift. And Eben would never, ever forget that, as long as he lived.

"Ach, I am happy to help," he said, and he meant it. "Aught that you need. Always."

17

In all Eben's wildest fantasies about Tryggr, he had never once imagined the bizarre, surreal experience of sitting across from Tryggr in his family's *hellir*, and listening intently to his Skai tale of woe.

It turned out that Alma, Drafli, and Baldr had bitterly quarrelled, to the point where Alma was now convalescing in the sickroom, and Baldr had run off above ground, alone. This had put Drafli in the highly unenviable position of needing to choose between them, and he had finally taken off after Baldr, after leaving detailed instructions with his clanmates about Alma—who, apparently, was now also pregnant with their son.

"But now *she*'s planning to run off again too!" Tryggr continued, his voice more agitated than Eben had ever heard it. "An' all those meddling Ash-Kai are supporting it as some kinda grand scheme—'cause her old fool boss is still rattling his swords at us, saying we kidnapped her, so if she goes back to him, he can't blame us anymore! An' I ken I should follow her, keep an eye on her like I have been, but just before he left"—Tryggr dragged both hands against his hair—"Boss told me to stay stuck here on my arse, *again*, and fix up the scullery! Make it real nice and new for her, he said!"

It was taking Eben's full concentration to follow all this, a task made all the more difficult by the unsettling anxiety in Tryggr's scent, and the pleading, beseeching look in his eyes. As if expecting Eben to solve all this for him at once, and Eben had to close his own eyes, draw in more of that sweet, reassuring scent, with still only him in it.

"But would Drafli not have considered all this, before he left?" Eben asked, as steadily as he could. "He has seemed to... *come around* on Alma, as you said he would, ach? He cares for her, does he not? Mayhap even"—his thoughts flicked back to that scent on Drafli's mouth—"welcomed her? Longed for her?"

Tryggr gave a heavy exhale, and jerked a distracted nod. "Ach, sure he does," he said thickly. "How could he not? She's sweet, loyal, works hard, wishes to please. *You* ought to know this, ach?"

There was a strangely accusatory tone in his voice, his eyes suddenly dark on Eben's face, and Eben blinked, and again fought to think. "Well, it seems to me," he began carefully, "that Drafli would not have failed to consider all this—most of all if Alma is now pregnant with their son. Would he not have spoken to the Ash-Kai of this? And you said he gave orders to your other Skai kin also, ach? You have many strong scouts and warriors amongst you, do you not?"

Tryggr grimaced, frowning at the floor, and again Eben felt a sudden surge of commiseration, of understanding. Tryggr clearly wanted to win his Boss's approval, wanted to show himself a strong and capable Skai—and here he'd been left behind again, trapped in a scullery, doing dull, tedious work he didn't feel was important.

"I ken this work has not been easy for you," Eben continued, steadier now, his eyes intent on Tryggr's face. "But amidst it, you have again and again shown Drafli he can trust you. You have kept his woman safe, you have granted her much help, you have offered her laughter and relief. You have been a good, faithful Skai. You have done much good work, sir."

The *sir* had slipped out before Eben had caught it, and though he winced, he kept his gaze steady on Tryggr's unreadable face. "Drafli trusts you," he said firmly. "And if he again asked for your help in the scullery, I ken this means he trusts you in this, too. He knows you shall do this. He knows you shall do more good work with this."

There was an instant's silence from Tryggr, and then a slow, harsh exhale, his hand rubbing at his eyes. "But I still know fuck all about that curst scullery," he said heavily. "How the hell am I s'posed to fix it up for her, and show Boss I can pull it off, if I can't even..."

But his voice had slowly trailed off, his eyes narrowing toward Eben's face. And Eben twitched a shy, sheepish smile back, even as a distant, disbelieving part of him wondered if Drafli hadn't known how this would unfold. Surely the most fearsome orc in the mountain didn't pay that much heed to what went on in the scullery... did he?

"You can," Eben told Tryggr, the conviction quiet but sure in his voice. "For we shall fix the scullery, and help your Boss, and your kin. Together."

18

Eben wasted no time in hustling Tryggr up to the scullery, and setting to work.

Tryggr still seemed a bit dazed by it all, casting Eben frequent narrow, searching glances, but Eben fought to stay focused on the task at hand. On helping Tryggr, and being a friend.

"First of all, I ken we could polish the counters and floors, to make these smoother, and easier to clean," he said firmly, as he glanced around at the now-empty scullery. "We could also install new, stronger drying racks, for these ones are not safe, ach? Most of all for a pregnant woman, and soon an orcling. And"—he dropped his gaze to the old wooden washbasins—"we could forge new steel basins, mayhap. And I could seek to finish plans for this washing machine I spoke of, also."

Tryggr was fully staring at Eben now, his swallow visibly bobbing in his throat. "You actually... set to work, on that whole washing machine idea?" he asked. "Don't recall giving you much encouragement at the time, did I?"

Eben flushed and waved it away, though he couldn't quite meet Tryggr's eyes. "I wished to help you," he said, too quickly.

"I ken this work has not always been easy for you. Most of all when you are such a fierce, fearsome warrior."

Tryggr blinked at him, and Eben was vaguely surprised to see a flush of red, creeping up his neck. "Uh, well, how long d'you think it'll all take, then?" he asked, with a curt wave between Eben and the room. "Forgot to tell you, Boss told me to spend whatever I need off his accounts, too."

Truly? Eben had already been uneasily recalling how much trouble his Ka-esh kin had given him over the floor-cleaning project, and he felt himself brightening, beaming at Tryggr's face. "That will be a great help," he replied. "And it is another sign of how much Drafli trusts you, is it not?"

The redness was spreading higher up Tryggr's neck, but he twitched a brief, grateful smile toward Eben, before lurching for the door. "Ach, then," he said, a little hoarse. "To the Ka-esh wing, then? But mayhap a stop by the sickroom first? See what's going on with Boss's woman?"

Eben nodded and warmly smiled back—he'd been about to suggest the same—and upon reaching the sickroom, they found it caught in a bustle of activity. It turned out that a morose but flinty-eyed Alma was indeed preparing to leave the mountain, and she had a variety of Ash-Kai and Grisk orcs hovering around her, all seemingly speaking at once. But lurking far more quietly near the door were two Skai orcs Eben now recognized, thanks to his previous observations—the lean scout Killik, and the huge, hulking warrior Ulfarr. Both of them obviously intending to accompany Alma on her journey, and Eben could feel Tryggr's shoulders sagging as he looked at them, and then signed something akin to, *You here for Boss? Watch over Alma?*

Killik's nod was curt and decisive, his hand signing back so swiftly that Eben couldn't fully follow it. But he could see Tryggr relaxing a little more at the sight of it, and then signing back slower, perhaps even so Eben could understand. *Thanks, brother. We'll have the scullery real nice for when you and Boss bring her back.*

Oh. So not only were these Skai joining Alma on her journey, but they were fully planning to return her in short order. And without at all meaning to, Eben reached and squeezed Tryggr's hand, and flashed him another swift, beaming smile.

Tryggr's glance toward Eben was grateful, his hand squeezing back, his claws gently prodding into Eben's skin. A sensation that had Eben twitching all over, heat pooling in his trousers—and it was enough to get him through a tearful goodbye with Alma, who seemed miserably unaware that she would very soon be returning.

"Thank you so much for all your help," she said, wiping at her eyes as she gave a weepy smile between Tryggr and Eben. "You've both been so wonderful."

The sight and scent of her sadness nearly had Eben weeping, too, and he was grateful when Tryggr managed most of the speaking, and then steered him out of the room. "Ach, naught to fret over, Ka-esh," Tryggr said firmly, with a little shake to his shoulder. "You were right that Boss has it all sorted out—Killik says he'll be boggled if she's away for more than a few days. So no need to scent thus, ach?"

Eben sniffed and nodded, aiming a grateful smile toward Tryggr's face—but Tryggr was frowning again, his eyes fixed to the corridor up ahead, his steps quickening on the stone floor. Perhaps just focused on how they apparently had a far shorter timeline than they'd anticipated, and Eben forced his attention back to the next tasks at hand. First collecting his own notes from his room, and then heading over to the engineers' *hellir*. Where, as expected, his former colleagues were initially highly reluctant to offer their support, but Eben countered their whining and demurring by offering shocking amounts of Drafli's coin, which soon sent several engineers scurrying for the scullery.

Next was a consultation with the construction and masonry teams, and after that was the forge, where Gareth instantly came out to meet them. His familiar genial face was flushed with heat from the ovens, his muscled arms and chest gleaming with sweat, and though he listened attentively to Eben's explanation, Eben didn't miss his frequent narrow glances toward Tryggr. Who, to Eben's vague surprise, was standing far closer to him than necessary, and frowning straight back toward Gareth, too.

"That fucking smith," Tryggr muttered afterwards, once Gareth had willingly agreed to work on the washbasins. "Skai-kesh above, I ken he'd do anything you asked, Ka-esh. An' then kneel and beg you for more."

What? Eben huffed a distracted, incredulous laugh, and shook his head. "Ach, no," he said, with a dismissive wave of his hand. "I am sure he would not. He wishes for someone who is a match for him. Someone... stronger."

His voice only slightly wavered as he spoke, angling a sheepish smile toward Tryggr's face, but Tryggr was studying him with sudden, surprising seriousness in his eyes. "You *are* strong, Ka-esh," he said flatly. "Strong, and brave, and true. One of the strongest orcs I've ever met."

What? The words struck Eben to stillness, right in the middle of the corridor, and Tryggr stopped too, flashing Eben a smile that didn't at all reach his eyes. "An' I bet you every one of my daggers, that smith misses you like hell right now," he continued, quieter, with a hollow little laugh. "Didn't realize how damn good he had it, ach?"

Eben couldn't seem to stop staring at Tryggr, breathing hard, while something knocked and swayed in his chest. Tryggr didn't... mean anything by that. Did he? He couldn't. He'd said he couldn't, he'd said he'd wanted a break from Eben. He'd said he'd seen it happen with his fathers, whatever *it* meant, but then... Tryggr had still come back, this morning. He was still here. As if...

"Gareth is only a friend," Eben finally replied, his voice a croak, his eyes holding to Tryggr's face. "Naught more. He is not... what I long for."

But wait, perhaps even that was too much, because something had darkened in Tryggr's eyes, and his scent suddenly tasted sharp, almost bitter. "Ach, I ken, Ka-esh," he said grimly. "I ken."

Well. Eben couldn't find a response to that, his stomach plummeting, his gaze dropping to the floor. Tryggr had made himself clear, yet again, and as much as it hurt, Eben had promised to help. To be a friend.

"Mayhap we ought to start cleaning the scullery next, then," he said, through his closed-off throat. "Ought to move out the laundry, before the masons begin sanding."

Tryggr didn't argue, and soon they'd rounded up a few more helpers, too—Duff, Gaukr, Timo, Gegnir, and even Alma's cat. And as they set to work cleaning, Eben did his best to keep smiling, being a friend, offering whatever support he could. Directing the Ka-esh masons when they arrived, liaising with Gareth and the engineers, and scrubbing laundry until his arms ached. Until finally Tryggr ordered him to bed, to which Eben blearily nodded, and then almost staggered straight into a wall.

"Ach, Ka-esh!" Tryggr yelped, and oh, that was his strong arm around Eben's shoulders, steering him toward the Ka-esh wing. And Eben willingly leaned into Tryggr's sweet-scented shoulder, his face shamefully tilting closer as Tryggr marched him down to his familiar room.

"D'you really *like* sleeping all the way down here in this hole?" Tryggr demanded, as he gently set Eben down on the bed, and then frowned around at the small room. "Not even close to the rest of your kin, is it? Or the library, if you need more books?"

Eben was far too weary to dissemble, and he shook his head. "I only came here because my father threw me out," he said, with a hollow laugh. "It was the furthest liveable room from our *hellir*, and I have been here ever since. But"—he shrugged, gave Tryggr a tired smile—"it is dark, at least, and quiet. I could not bear sleeping in a place like the sickroom or the Grisk wing, ach? Full of noise, and *lamps*."

He couldn't hide his shudder, followed by a regretful wince, because the lamps were important, they were there for the women who needed them—but to his vague surprise, Tryggr grimaced too, and nodded. "Couldn't bear it either," he said, as he nudged Eben's shoulder down toward the bed. "Glad Boss has kept some parts of the Skai wing dark for us."

Eben wistfully sighed and nodded—the Skai wing had been very cozy, and far more conveniently located, too—and curled up on his bed, as Tryggr draped a fur over him. And it was so easy to sink into sleep with Tryggr there, even if just for a moment...

The next day was full of even more intensive labour in the scullery, first cleaning up all the dust from the masons, and then helping to prepare the wall for the new drying racks, while continuing to work through the last of the laundry. Eben also made several stops by the sickroom, mixing up any necessary prescriptions as quickly as he could, until Tryggr again appeared, and marched him off to bed. But this time, instead of taking Eben down to the Ka-esh wing, Tryggr steered him... up. Up, into the far nearer Skai wing, down one of those cozy curling corridors, into a room that scented of... him.

It was small but clean, with a large fur-covered bed, several thick fur rugs, and multiple glinting weapons lining the walls. And Eben willingly sank onto the soft, sweet-scented bed, even as he blinked blankly at Tryggr's unreadable face.

"But this is—your room?" he asked, too tentative, because what was this, why had Tryggr brought him here—and Tryggr nudged him over on the bed, before dropping his own fully clothed body down beside Eben.

"You've been working your pretty little arse off on this project for me, Ka-esh," Tryggr said flatly. "Want you to at least get a good night's rest, away from that godsforsaken hole of yours."

Oh. Eben was again far too tired to argue, and he might have even leaned a little closer into Tryggr's warm body, inhaling the deep, rich sweetness of his scent. "Thank you, sir," he murmured, before he could stop it. "You have been so good to me."

Tryggr made a faint scoffing sound, but oh, that was his arm, nudging under Eben's head. Meaning that Eben could rest his head on Tryggr's shoulder, breathe in the beautiful scent of him for an entire night, and it made for sweet, wonderful dreams, full of home and safety and longing.

When Eben awoke again, it was to the feel of Tryggr shifting out of bed, and striding toward the door. Toward where the huge Skai Ulfarr was waiting, and darting a brief, narrow look at Eben in the bed. "Boss is headed back now, with both his mates," he told Tryggr, in a deep, flat voice. "Is this scullery ready for his woman? I ken he wishes it as part of his mating-gift to her."

Wait. Drafli had... taken Alma as his *mate*? As in, he'd sworn *vows* to her? And he'd meant the scullery project as part of his *mating-gift*?

Eben could feel the surprise flashing across Tryggr's scent, and then something almost like relief. Or even like pride, billowing brief and bright, because his Boss had trusted him with something as important as a mating-gift. And his nod toward Ulfarr was quick and jaunty, even as his eyes glanced back at Eben in the bed, lingering longer than Eben might have expected.

"Ach, we're almost done," he told Ulfarr. "You ken you can count on me, brother."

Ulfarr nodded in return, and even gave a brief little bow toward Tryggr before turning away again. Making it clear that he—and surely by extension, Drafli, and the Skai—did know they could count on Tryggr. That in taking on this project, Tryggr had again proven he could be trusted. And maybe— maybe Eben had proven he could be a friend, too.

Eben couldn't help a shy, genuine smile toward Tryggr, and then—foolish—a little bow of his own, too, his hand over his heart. And why was Tryggr still looking at him like that, slowly prowling back across the room toward the bed, his hand reaching out, his claws tickling at Eben's neck...

The room suddenly felt very hot, Tryggr's scent far too strong and rich in the air—and oh, hell, that was a distinct swell at the front of Tryggr's trousers, too. Suggesting, hinting, offering, and Eben's mouth was watering, his tongue brushing his lips, his eyes rising hungry and beseeching to Tryggr's unreadable face...

But no, wait, *no*, Tryggr had said he didn't want that from Eben. He'd been very, very clear, and a true friend would respect that, and honour that. So Eben gritted his teeth, forced his eyes downwards, fought to draw in breath. "We do not have much time, then," he croaked. "I ought to go see about the basins, mayhap."

There was an instant's stillness, too thick in the choked air—and then Tryggr's hand dropped from Eben's neck, his body spinning away, his hands running against where his hair had half-fallen out of its topknot. "Ach," he said flatly. "I must go—wash. Meet you in the scullery?"

Eben jerked a nod that Tryggr didn't see, because he'd already dodged out the door. Leaving Eben sitting there alone, breathing hard, his hands in fists, his cock helplessly straining in his trousers. He was being a friend. A friend. That was all.

But he had to drag himself out of that lovely, sweet-scented room, and on to the day's work. First was to the sickroom, where he quickly washed up and consulted with Efterar before mixing the day's prescriptions. And next was down to the Ka-esh forge, where Gareth had begun assembling and testing the two new washing machines. "Ach, they shall be ready this afternoon, brother," Gareth firmly told him. "Naught to fear."

The reassurance didn't seem to have nearly the same effect as it did when Tryggr gave it, and Eben twitched a distracted nod, and rushed back up to the scullery. To where a team of Ka-esh builders were now installing the new drying racks, while Tryggr mopped the newly polished floor, Timo and Gegnir scrubbed the walls and counters, and Duff and Gaukr addressed the day's new laundry.

But by noon, Duff and Gaukr—whose romance had continued apace—had begun darting lingering glances at each other, the scents of their hunger spiking powerfully through the air. Until finally Tryggr threw up his hands, and ordered them off into Alma's back office, leaving Tryggr and Eben to finish the laundry together, alone. Both of them purposefully not looking at one another until what must have been late afternoon, when a sweaty Killik appeared at the scullery door, signed something at Tryggr, and left again.

"Ach, Boss and his mates are almost back!" Tryggr exclaimed, breathless. "Are we almost done? Where's the washing machines?"

His voice sounded unnaturally shrill, his eyes almost panicked, and Eben couldn't help a reflexive squeeze at his arm, and his most hopeful, reassuring smile. "I shall fetch them," he said. "Whilst you take the others, and greet your Boss and his mates. Show them how well you have done, and how right they were to trust you."

Tryggr's breath exhaled heavy and slow, his head nodding, his eyes intent and grateful on Eben's face. "Thanks, Ka-esh," he said gruffly. "Couldn'a done it without you. You've been— brilliant. The best."

Oh. Well. And again, Eben felt himself smiling, slow and genuine, as the contentment settled deep in his belly. He'd done it. He'd been a friend. He'd done—good work.

He could trust a Skai, and he could also trust... himself.

"Thank you, sir," he said to Tryggr, without dropping his eyes, without even a hitch in his voice. "I was happy to help."

19

Washing machines, Eben soon discovered, were far heavier than they had any right to be.

He found help carrying the first one up to the scullery, thanks to a kind Bautul—a former patient—who had taken pity on his plight. But the second one felt almost twice as heavy as the first, and by the time Eben reached the scullery, he was sweaty and staggering on his feet, and cursing himself for not thinking to have procured a cart.

"Ach, Ka-esh!" Tryggr exclaimed, upon catching sight of Eben at the scullery door—and he instantly rushed over, snatching the washer from Eben's twitching arms, and setting it onto one of the steel basins. "Watch yourself, Ka-esh. Or call for help when you need it, ach?"

There was true alarm in his scent, studding deep into Eben's belly, but this time it felt almost easy to smile back, despite the heat surging into his cheeks. "Sorry, sir," he replied, wincing even as it came out of his mouth—friends, *friends*— and he forced his gaze back up, away, toward the other scents in the room. And yes, here was Duff, and Gegnir, and Alma herself. Alma's pretty face was flushed and eager, her scent bright with delighted happiness—suggesting, surely, that she was pleased with their work on the scullery. She also reeked of both Drafli and Baldr's fresh scents, even stronger and deeper than before. Proving that they had indeed settled matters between them, and brought her home again, for good.

If she can keep it up, show Boss she's worth his time, I ken he'll come around.

"And welcome back, Keeper," Eben shyly told her, as that familiar envious longing caught low in his belly. "We are glad you are home again."

Alma beamed back at him, while beside her, Tryggr loudly cleared his throat, and kicked at the new washbasin. "Well, don't keep her in suspense, Ka-esh," he said flatly. "Show her how it works, will you?"

Right. Eben's face flushed even hotter, but he quickly nodded and bent over the basin. "This is a washing machine," he explained, as his trembling hand found the handle, and gave it a careful turn. "We had heard of them being used in the north, and it is a simple concept, so we made our own, ach? You turn the handle, and the paddle beneath shall wash your clothes for you."

He turned it again, demonstrating how the large paddle swung through the basin below. A sight that sparked genuine awe in Alma's eyes and scent, so Eben waved her forward, and smiled as she gave it a tentative turn, too.

"It's brilliant," she fervently said, with a bright, grateful smile over her shoulder toward him. "And so well crafted, too. This will save us so much time. Thank you."

Eben waved it away, but the envious longing had slightly faded again, sinking into a deep, genuine contentment. He'd been a friend. He'd done good work. He had.

"Ach, I was happy to help," he said, and he meant it. "We all wish you to feel welcome, and stay."

There was an instant's tense, awkward silence, during

which Alma blushed, and something dark and almost angry flashed through Tryggr's scent. Something that felt depressingly familiar at this point, because Eben had scented it on him so many times before—and as he blinked at Tryggr's frowning face, it distantly occurred to him that it had so often happened around... Alma. Except for that awful moment outside the Skai arena, perhaps, when Tryggr had scented just like this, and said, *I know what you really want. I just... can't. I've seen Pa and Pabbi go through it, my whole fucking life, and I'm not gonna...*

A strange, sudden suspicion had begun flaring in Eben's chest, while Tryggr's stiff body shifted, his eyes narrow on Eben's, his jaw flexing tight in his cheek. His breath drawing in, his shoulders pulling up, as if he was about to say...

"Maybe you haven't noticed, Ka-esh," Tryggr said, his voice hard. "But this woman's spoken for. Permanently."

Oh. Wait. *Wait.* Tryggr thought Eben was... what? That Eben was trying to... with *Alma*?!

Eben blinked, stared at Tryggr's grim, flinty eyes, tasted the bitter darkness in his scent—and suddenly it was as though time had frozen, halted, flashing wild shocked disbelief up Eben's spine, while memories marched behind his eyes. Memories of every time he'd spoken about Alma to Tryggr, spoken to Alma around Tryggr—and how Eben's own damned envy and longing had also been there, thick and choking in his scent. Telling Tryggr... *I want this. I long for this. I long for... her.*

Tryggr had scented Eben's envy, and he'd thought it meant Eben wanted Alma. A *woman.*

And now Tryggr's words—his distress—from outside the arena seemed to snap into a new light, too. *I just can't,* he'd said, *I've seen Pa and Pabbi go through it*—just as Eben had witnessed it with so many orcs, too. Becoming attached to an orc who truly wanted a woman was a path straight to misery, and no wonder Tryggr hadn't wanted that, Eben certainly didn't want it either, but had—had Tryggr really thought that, all this time?

But yes, yes, that scent was still there on Tryggr, deepening by the breath—and now that Eben was breathing it, looking at it, it did scent so much like... envy. Like jealousy. Like the same hopeless, helpless longing he knew far, far too well.

And curse it, Alma and Duff and Gegnir were still all standing here watching, listening, and Eben had to try. Had to say something, something that wouldn't insult Alma, something that wasn't *Of course I don't want her, I barely noticed her, I want you, you, you...*

But no, wait, maybe Eben was still wrong on this, too. Maybe he was still seeing what he wanted to see, from someone who he'd sworn to treat as a friend. And he needed to give Tryggr a way out, too, needed to offer a way for him to say no, to pretend none of this had ever happened—and curse it, what even had Tryggr said? *Maybe you haven't noticed, Ka-esh, but this woman's spoken for. Permanently.*

"Ach, I—I ken," Eben finally stammered, into the taut, waiting silence. "She has gained the most fearsome Skai in our mountain as her lord. Through not her beauty or her strength, but through"—he drew in a shaky breath—"her hard work. Her kindness."

And maybe it had still been foolish, or insulting, or betraying too much—but Eben trusted Tryggr, he did. They were still—friends. And that wasn't confusion or mockery flashing through Tryggr's eyes, lighting up his scent. No, no, it was...

Shock. Relief. Longing. And a slow, stunning smile, curling dark and delighted on his lips.

A smile that said, *I see. I see you. I can show you the way.*

"Is that so, pretty Ka-esh?" Tryggr said, his voice far lower, huskier, as the dizzying scent of his hunger blazed raw and reckless through the air. "You like the idea of catching a hungry Skai's eye, do you?"

Oh. Oh. Eben's breath escaped in a noiseless little whimper, his eyes wide and arrested on Tryggr's face. And he could taste his own yearning, tangled up with that same envy and greed, as his prick swelled to instant hardness in his trousers. A sight Tryggr certainly hadn't missed, his bright eyes darting downward, as his scent burned with gleeful satisfaction. With... *triumph.*

Eben only vaguely noticed Duff and Gegnir leaving the room, because Tryggr had already begun to prowl closer toward him, his steps slow and silent on the stone floor, his claws jutting sharp from his fingers. "Then why don't you bend over, little Ka-esh, and show us this again," he said, kicking his boot at the washbasin. "Give us a better look this time, ach?"

Oh, hell. He didn't mean it, he didn't, he couldn't—but the command was ringing in his eyes, in his heated hungry scent. *I see you. I can show you the way.*

Bend over.

Eben's body shuddered all over, the hope and hunger and longing choking raw and riotous into his scent. Tryggr couldn't truly want this, this couldn't be happening—but Tryggr was still here, watching him, waiting for his answer. And Eben trusted Tryggr, he trusted this Skai, *I can show you the way...*

So with a gulp and a shiver, Eben turned around, and obeyed.

20

In all his years visiting the *dýflissa*, Eben had never felt so bared, so exposed, as in this moment. Standing bent double and shivering over a washbasin in a scullery, with his still-clothed arse jutting up for anyone to see. For Tryggr to see.

There was a moment's choked stillness as Eben kept standing there, waiting, quivering, please—but then, oh, Tryggr's hands. Tryggr's warm, capable hands, touching Eben, smoothing against his trembling hips. And oh, oh, with a flick of his fingers, the drawstring on Eben's trousers loosened, sagging the waistband downward—and now Tryggr was drawing the trousers down too, baring Eben even further, right here in the damned scullery.

It was against the rules, Eben's distant thoughts shouted, and Alma was still standing there watching it, scenting of stunned disbelief—but oh, Eben had never known such violent, desperate need, crashing through him, clawing him from the inside out. Tryggr was touching him. Tryggr was undressing him. Tryggr wanted to see what was his. Tryggr wanted... *him*.

"Ach, just like that," Tryggr's low voice purred from behind Eben, his scent hot, sweet, approving, as Eben's trousers dropped around his ankles. "You *are* eager to please, aren't you?"

Eben's face was burning, his bare upraised arse trembling in the cool open air—but he somehow nodded, yes, of course he was, *yes*. And Tryggr rewarded it with a leisurely stroke of his warm hand, sliding over the curve of Eben's arse. The touch soft, gentle, but for the sharp, succulent scrape of his claws, dragging against Eben's bare, tingling skin.

"Ach, just as I thought," Tryggr continued, his voice even lower. "So pretty, Ka-esh. Bet you're nice and tight too, ach?"

Oh, yes, yes, Eben could be, he would be, please, and Tryggr's hungry hand was already slipping closer, sliding slow and deliberate into Eben's crease. And this wasn't happening, it couldn't be happening... but yes, Eben could feel a single finger deftly seeking, settling against his quivering rim—and then—

Pressing. Prodding gentle but firm, pushing into Eben's body with brazen, proprietary ease. As if Tryggr had every right to finger him like this, to feel him like this, right here in the scullery, while Alma watched—and he did have every right, he *did*, and it was all Eben could do to stay upright, to remember how to breathe.

"You ever take a Skai in here before, Ka-esh?" Tryggr murmured, dark and hot, as his finger kept prodding, searching, sinking all the way to the knuckle. "Ever have a strong Skai ploughing, and get pumped full of good Skai seed?"

Fuck. Eben's moan choked from his mouth, his invaded body frantically pulsing around that impossible finger, and he couldn't stop his back from arching, his bared, opened arse pushing back harder, deeper. Needing more, more, desperate and shameful, and behind him, Tryggr gave a low, husky laugh, and—oh, *hell*—a gentle slap of his other hand at Eben's arse-cheek.

"Ach, ach, you'll get it," Tryggr drawled, and oh, Eben could feel him shifting, could hear the sound of rustling fabric. As if—as if Tryggr was dropping his trousers. As if he was truly going to fuck Eben, to plough him full of good Skai seed, here, now, please, please...

"You're gonna suck me all the way inside you, aren't you, pretty Ka-esh?" Tryggr continued, as that finger slowly slid out of Eben, making him whimper with displeasure as it slipped free—but oh, now that was the sweet, stunning scent of Tryggr's fresh seed, the slick sound of a swift pumping hand. "Show me what a good little pet you could be?"

Oh. Oh, oh, please, Eben's brain was distantly dancing and screeching, his heart lurching into his throat, his body trembling so hard he nearly lost his footing. But he was nodding, nodding, arching up, opening as wide as he could. Waiting, showing Tryggr, he could be such a good pet, please...

And then—a touch. A touch, slick and blunt and warm, pressing against Eben's twitching, waiting arse. It was Tryggr, Tryggr's prick was touching him, Tryggr's prick wanted to fuck him—and Eben instantly bore down, opened wider. Relaxing enough to let that thick, solid flesh push into him, breach into him, stretching him out around it...

And once it was fully in, its head eased just past the muscle, Eben clamped it tight. Squeezing as hard as he could, giving them both that sweet drag and friction, and he could feel Tryggr's prick instantly vibrating fuller, his hands spasming against Eben's hips. While he just kept sinking deeper, and deeper, perhaps halfway inside now, Tryggr was inside Eben, he was fucking him in the scullery, fucking him in front of the woman he'd thought Eben had really wanted.

And wait, perhaps there was something in that, some kind of test on Tryggr's part, or even more of that triumph—and curse him, but Eben couldn't help a brief, darting glance up toward Alma. Toward where she was already staring straight back at him, her face red, her scent reeking of shock and incredulity, and—Eben blinked—just a twitch of envy, too.

"Tryggr!" Alma hissed, as she shook her head, and clapped her shaky hands over her eyes. "You can't just go ahead and—"

But Tryggr had surely caught that scent on her too, and oh, Eben could feel Tryggr's upper body bending forward, shifting his cock a little deeper, so he could inhale at Eben's neck. Seeking Eben's own jealousy or envy, perhaps—but there was only the wheeling charging hunger, and perhaps a shudder of his own triumph, too. Tryggr was fucking him. *Him.* And of course Eben hadn't wanted Alma, he wanted this, only this, and if Alma had thought otherwise, well, then she could watch and learn the truth for herself. She could watch Eben take a Skai's gorgeous prick, see how pretty he was, see what a good pet he could be...

Tryggr's deep inhale had shuddered into a laugh, low and gleeful, his breath tickling against Eben's neck. And that was another light, gentle slap of his hand to Eben's arse, speaking of hunger, of approval. Saying, surely, *I scent you. I see you. I can show you the way.*

"Ach, sure I can," Tryggr told Alma as he stood tall behind Eben again, his hand now palming possessively at Eben's arse-cheek. "Boss had you in here while we watched, didn't he? And it seems to me this Ka-esh likes it just as much as you did—and he even likes you watching, too. Don't you, my pretty pet?"

Another slap struck against Eben's arse, shuddering him all over, and there was no thought, no hesitation, only nodding, agreeing, obeying. "Ach," he croaked. "Sir."

The scent of Tryggr's triumph bloomed stronger through the air, and his laugh sounded breathless this time, his hand giving Eben's arse an approving little squeeze. "Then see, woman, you ought not deny him this," he said smugly. "Most of all after he has shown you such kindness."

It was unthinkable, impossible, even that Tryggr could keep

speaking like this, arguing like this, while Eben was helplessly panting and trembling beneath him, pinioned upon his cock. But perhaps that was part of the triumph too, and part of why Tryggr so blatantly wanted Alma to see this. Wanting her to witness him staking his claim, on both Eben and maybe even the whole damned room, just like Drafli had done with Alma. Making it clear exactly how this stood—and it was with Eben bent over a washing machine, with Tryggr's prick stuck halfway up his arse.

Eben could taste Alma's resignation, and thankfully her amusement, too—and finally she dropped her hands from her eyes, and gave Tryggr a wry, tolerant smile. And yes, yes, that was what Tryggr had wanted, and the scent of his triumph bubbled even higher as his firm hands caressed Eben's flanks, and that invading cock finally, finally resumed its slow, steady plunge inside him.

"Ach, that's it," Tryggr's low voice breathed, as he leisurely pushed his way through Eben's tight dragging clutch. "That's nice, little Ka-esh, real nice. Good and tight and sweet, ach?"

Oh, *yes*, and Eben whimpered and shivered as that hot driving head bumped up against solid flesh—but with a moan, he purposefully shifted and softened, and opened that, too. Welcoming Tryggr deeper, as deep as he could go, *you're gonna suck me all the way inside you, show me what a good little pet you could be...*

Tryggr's breath choked as he pressed further, carefully sinking himself even deeper within, into the double lock of Eben's grip. Until his hips ground up flush against Eben's arse, because oh, he was in, he'd filled Eben with Skai, opened him up as wide and deep as he could go. And Eben was squeezing as hard as he could, seizing and spasming against his lord, showing him what a good pet he would be, please...

"Just like that," Tryggr rasped, as his hips began gently

grinding, circling, gouging himself even deeper. "Even better than I thought. *Ach.*"

The pleasure and the frenzy were everywhere, everything, and Eben couldn't stop his moans, his body arching up, pressing back, needing more—when something caught, gentle but firm, at his braid. Tryggr's hand, holding it, drawing Eben's head back, as he slowly, deliberately drew his cock out, away, breath by agonizing breath. Adding just a perfect twinge of pain to the dizzying loss, reminding Eben who was in control, in charge, *you'll get it, I can show you the way...*

Tryggr slammed back inside with one smooth, staggering stroke, driving through Eben's tight grip, seating himself hard and deep. Hurling out more fierce, fizzing pleasure, with just that beautiful painful edge, and Eben writhed and shouted beneath it, lost in it, *please.*

"You like that too, little Ka-esh?" came Tryggr's low, hoarse voice behind him. "You like your Skai being a bit rough with you? Making sure you feel it?"

Fuck, yes, and Eben frantically nodded, while a distant rational part of him shivered with warmth, with happiness. Because Tryggr knew Eben liked it rough, of course he knew, but he was still—asking. Still making sure Eben wanted that from him. Showing Eben, again, that he could be trusted, even when he was fucking his arse in a scullery.

And Tryggr was pleased too, his chuckle low and approving as he ground himself deeper, and leisurely began wrapping Eben's braid around his hand. Increasing the tension, giving it an experimental tug, scenting for any pain or misery—but it was perfect, perfect. And Tryggr knew it, keeping that throbbing smarting sweetness as he slowly drew out again, holding it for a hanging, hovering breath...

"Even better, little Ka-esh," he said, dark and low, as he slammed back inside, even more forceful than before. Making Eben shout and flail beneath it, his hair pulling against Tryggr's iron grip, his body clamping tight and desperate against the invasion of that wondrous, pulsing Skai cock.

"Ach, you're so pretty, aren't you?" Tryggr asked, as he drew out again, drove back in. "So sweet, when you're being railed by a good Skai prick?"

Yes, please, Tryggr was railing Eben now, ramming in again and again, yanking his head back harder, as his other hand's sharp claws dragged against Eben's hip. And Eben was lost, consumed, in the furious frenzied euphoria of it, in all his hunger and longing and fantasy made truth by this orc, this perfect orc, his friend, his trust, his home.

"So sweet," Tryggr gasped again, his voice catching, his hips plunging harder, wrenching the pleasure hotter and wilder between them. "And you're gonna smell even sweeter when you're chock-full of Skai seed, aren't you? When you're walking around here reeking of *me*?"

Fuck, yes, yes, yes, Tryggr's bollocks tightening against Eben's crease, his cock swelling, straining, locking in place— and then he groaned, guttural and deep, as he sprayed out deep inside. Pouring Eben full of that hot Skai seed, flooding him from the bottom up, as those sharp claws dug into his hip, yanking at his hair—

It was so much, so much, so perfect, everything—and without even a touch, Eben's own cock shuddered, and then sprayed out, too. Releasing its pent-up longing again and again, spurting out in thick, heavy-scented strings. Catching all over Gareth's new washing machine beneath him, painting it with his pleasure, while the ecstasy screamed and screamed through his body, his head, his heart.

By the end of it, Eben was shuddering almost too much to stand, his entire body tingling and shivering with the aftershocks, but Tryggr was still here, holding him upright. Both his hands now gripping firmly at Eben's hips, while his still-hard cock held safe and deep inside, and the taste of his own pleasure and relief kept whirling, flooding heavy and reassuring through the air. Saying, without a doubt, that he'd liked it, too. Eben had pleased him. He had.

But then Tryggr cleared his throat, his hand palming possessive and a little rough at Eben's quivering arse. "Look at you, pretty pet," he murmured. "Messing all over your brand-new gift. You're gonna lick that clean for me now, aren't you?"

Oh, fuck. Eben's body spasmed at Tryggr's cock still inside him, and he was already nodding, his face burning, as he ducked his head, and obeyed. Licking at the too-strong taste of his own seed, sprayed all over Gareth's brand-new forging. And that was unquestionably another statement too, another very purposeful point made on Tryggr's part, putting Gareth in his place—and maybe putting Eben in his place, too. Showing him that this was how it would be, with Tryggr fucking him, commanding him, and covering over any claim Gareth might have had upon him.

And with Tryggr... approving of him. Caressing him, stroking him without claws, now, as a low, hungry moan hissed from his throat.

"That's good, pretty pet," he breathed, low and hot. "Real good. Now tell me, sweet thing"—he leaned forward, his lips gently brushing to the back of Eben's neck—"what's your name?"

Wait, what? Eben startled, breathless, and he only vaguely heard Alma's faint, disbelieving laugh as she finally headed for the door, closing it tightly behind her. While Tryggr's sweaty body shivered against Eben, and a low, regretful chuckle huffed against his skin.

"Never thought to ask you, pet," Tryggr continued, sounding suddenly almost—shy. "An' you never said, and by the time I realized, I didn't want to risk asking any of the others, either. Didn't want 'em to catch how attached I was getting to you, I ken."

Oh. Tryggr had done all that, all this, fucked Eben in a scullery, when he hadn't even known his *name*—but he was also softly kissing at Eben's neck, his hunger and regret shimmering through the air. *Didn't want 'em to catch how attached I was getting to you...*

"It's—Eben," he replied, in a rush, over his shaky breath. "Eben, of Clan Ka-esh."

He winced even as he said it, foolish, foolish, of course Tryggr knew his clan, right? But Tryggr's mouth was still kissing, his hands still caressing, his prick still slightly spasming deep inside. "Eben," he repeated, as if testing it, assessing it, just like he'd done with his finger in Eben's arse. "Eben, of Clan Ka-esh. It's a good name, pet. Real good."

Eben's shudder was fierce, far too conspicuous, but Tryggr's warm hands just kept stroking, rubbing it out, easing him back into steadiness again. "So you never wanted Boss's woman, then?" came Tryggr's voice, more careful than before. "Not even a little bit?"

Eben's head instantly shook back and forth, as a choked-sounding laugh escaped from his throat. "Ach, no," he croaked. "I was only—jealous. I wished for you to—notice me, and bring me joy, and... *come around.* As Drafli did with her."

And it was foolish again, shameful, but Tryggr's mouth just kept kissing his neck, warm hands steadily stroking at his sides. "An' what about other women, then?" Tryggr asked, and that sounded careful, too. "You long for one? Or a son?"

Eben's laugh was easy and incredulous this time, as his still-invaded arse gave a tight, sustained squeeze against Tryggr's solid flesh. "No," he breathed. "Never."

He could scent Tryggr's relief, could feel his heavy exhale on his neck. "Good, pet," he said, hoarse. "Never did much for me, either. Even tried a coupla times, even just to mayhap give Pa a grandson, but it never stuck, ach? Not like this."

Not like this. Like this, with his breath on Eben's neck, his prick in Eben's arse, his possessive hands stroking Eben's skin. And the sweet heady taste in his scent, the taste that somehow seemed so much stronger, unmarred by any of that darkness or jealousy. Hunger. Triumph. Affection. Awe.

"Shoulda just fucking asked," Tryggr went on, his voice slightly cracking. "Just thought—thought it was so clear in your scent, ach? An' I could scent how you liked me, too, so I thought—ach. Thought you might just tell me what we both wanted to hear, only for it to come haunt us later. Once I got myself too attached to stay away."

Eben couldn't seem to speak, but it was all shifting and settling in his thoughts, sinking into comprehension, or even sympathy. While Tryggr's breath shuddered against his neck, his hands gripping even tighter, as if to keep holding Eben here upon him, where he could never escape...

"But got too attached anyway," Tryggr whispered, with a broken little laugh. "Couldn't stand to hurt you, or keep away from you. You're so sweet, Ka-esh, so pretty, so fucking *perfect*."

What? Eben's disbelief finally cut through the shuddering warmth, his head rapidly shaking. "Ach, no," he gulped. "I am not, I am—"

But oh, those were Tryggr's claws, pricking into his skin. "Ach, you are," he insisted. "You're so damned clever. You know so much. You work so hard. You're devoted to helping all your kin, even if you have to put up with constant rubbish to do it. Ach, you've been so good and patient with Duff, when so many people barely even see him, let alone think he's worth talking to. He wouldn't stop asking"—Tryggr huffed a low laugh—"why I wasn't making you reek more of Skai, so you'd keep coming round, and helping us."

Eben's mouth twitched up, even though his head attempted another shake—but Tryggr's claws were digging in deeper, shuddering him to stillness. "An' you were loyal, too," he said, harder. "You coulda gone back to that dungeon, to that Gareth prick, any fucking time you wanted—but you didn't. You took my scent, and then kept it only mine, when you didn't need to. You—gave me that, Ka-esh, without me even asking. An' that means a lot, mayhap most of all to a Skai, ach?"

Right. Eben's thoughts had again flicked back to those old Skai rules, to Skai not offering fealty to other orcs. But clearly some of them still wanted it, like Drafli, and maybe... maybe now Tryggr, too.

"An' mayhap it's vain of me," Tryggr added, husky, "but I ken you're also the prettiest little thing I've ever seen in my life, ach? You're so pretty it hurts, Ka-esh, most of all when you blush and stammer like you do, and flutter your big eyes at me. An' then you say all the sweet things you do, and tell me you wanna honour me, and then you fucking just—bend over, and offer it up, too. You offer up this, give me this—but then you want me to take it, too? Want me to pound you, to get rough with you? To do whatever the hell I want with you? Make you beg and squeal and squirt for me?"

Fuck. Eben's own hunger was surging again, shuddering up between them, seizing him around Tryggr's prick—and Tryggr moaned, breathless, even as his hand gave Eben's arse another firm slap. "An' fucking *that*," he breathed. "Never felt anything like this tight little arse of yours, Ka-esh. Like it's just made to be fucked and filled by a good Skai prick. Just like"—he hissed, ground deeper—"that perfect mouth of yours, too. You ken what it did to me that day, to have your pretty head in my lap, your big eyes worshipping me, while I buried my prick in your tight little throat, and blasted my bollocks straight into your belly?"

Oh, hell. Eben's moan rasped from his mouth, his body clamping even tighter around Tryggr's invading prick. "Ach," he gasped, thoughtless, helpless. "It was—so good. All I ever— longed for."

Tryggr's answering groan was low and approving, his hips

steadily thrusting. Moving easier, now, slicker, because he'd already poured Eben so full of him—but oh, that made it even better, Tryggr's thick cock now gliding smooth and slippery against Eben's grip, his breath hitching against Eben's neck.

"So you're gonna be mine, ach, pretty pet?" Tryggr hissed, low and dangerous into Eben's throat, and oh, that was his hand, too, curling close and possessive around Eben's neck. "You're gonna sign over this tight little arse to me, and let me do whatever the hell I want with it?"

Fuck, yes, yes, please, and Eben was babbling it aloud, shuddering and staggering over the washbasin—but wait, Tryggr had hesitated, and his hand around Eben's neck softened. Cradling it, caressing it, as if it were something precious, something cherished.

"But you ken, Eben," he said, slower now, his voice careful on Eben's name. "You can always say no to me too, ach? An' me wanting to make you mine, take you as my pet, you ken it's more about—playing and fucking, ach? It's not about me seeing you as weak, or below me, naught like that. It's me knowing how damn good you are, how perfect you are, and wanting to—to honour you, and take good care of you, and keep you happy and safe. It means—I *care*. An' it means"—he exhaled, slow and shuddering—"I want to keep you, Eben. Want to care for you, as long as I can."

More warmth was shimmering and sparking, deep in Eben's very soul, and he had to fight to find words, to bring up truth. "I—want that too," he whispered, his eyes blinking hard. "I have wanted it for—so long. But ach, I have not wished to be foolish, or weak, or subservient, or—"

He swallowed hard, twitching his head back and forth, his father's distant voice rising—but Tryggr's mouth was kissing him again, his hand gently stroking his throat. "Ach, I ken," he murmured. "You deserve kindness, and honour, and respect. Deserve to have your wishes heard and followed and protected.

An' if some snippy Ash-Kai or fool Ka-esh starts barrelling over you, or giving you grief, you deserve to have your Skai backing you up and hurling daggers."

Oh. Oh, yes, oh please. And Eben truly couldn't speak now, not with the quivering happiness choking in his breath, escaping in a half-laugh, half-sob. And Tryggr huffed a low, relieved-sounding laugh too, his hand caressing harder against Eben's throat, his prick giving an experimental little grind inside.

"And you deserve a good Skai prick filling up your arse, don't you, pet?" Tryggr said, lower. "You deserve a strong Skai ploughing whenever you wish, ach?"

Yes, yes, and Eben frantically nodded, so hard he almost staggered sideways—but oh, Tryggr still had him safe, had him by the neck, and up the arse. "Good, pet," he growled, as he drew a little out, and sank back inside. "Real good. An' from now on, you're only gonna scent of me. No fucking careless Ka-esh, no shitty smiths, none of it. Just *me*."

Eben's nod came even faster, more fervent, wrenching his neck in Tryggr's grip, and oh, Tryggr rewarded it with a gentle prod of claws, a snap of his teeth in his ear. "An' you ken I'll take such good care of you, pet," he breathed. "I'll make you beg and scream and weep for me, as much as you damn well want. But"—he slammed in harder, deeper—"there'll be no fucking lashes in our bed, you ken? Nothing that puts you at risk, because you're *mine*, an' I *won't—fucking—allow it*."

He punctuated the words with stunning, juddering slams of his cock, his hand yanking up and sideways on Eben's braid, making Eben twist to look at him. And oh, fuck, how Tryggr looked, his eyes blazing, his teeth bared, his face flushed bright. And Eben could only nod, hold his gaze, squeeze that still-driving prick as fiercely as he could, yes, yes, *yes*.

"Yes, sir," he whispered, to those dangerous Skai eyes, his lashes fluttering. "Whatever you wish, sir."

And yes, yes, Tryggr's groan shook between them, his eyes rolling back as he gouged in, raw and ravenous and desperate—and then he sprayed out, again. Pouring Eben full of him, again, and this time, Eben somehow found the strength to clutch his own straining prick in hand, and pump out his own release, too. Spraying it even wider across Gareth's washer, covering it all over with his seed, seeping it into all the cracks and crevices. Ensuring it would always smell of this, of them, of Tryggr fucking out Eben's seed, and making him his own.

"Good, Ka-esh," Tryggr whispered, shaky into Eben's neck, as his teeth scraped over his skin. "Real good. You're gonna be such a good little pet, aren't you?"

And even as his teeth finally struck, sinking deep and hungry into Eben's skin, Eben could still feel him watching, waiting for the answer. Needing to hear it, even now, even as he greedily gulped Eben's lifeblood, and kept squeezing the dregs of his bollocks into Eben's belly.

"Ach, sir," Eben said, and he meant it, so deep it sang and ached in his heart. "I am honoured to serve."

21

When Tryggr finally finished with Eben in the scullery, Eben was flushed and sweaty and rumpled all over, his hair mussed and loose, his marked neck streaked and sticky with his blood. And his legs were still weak and shaky, his arse rough and raw, to the point where he was noticeably limping, and clinging tightly to Tryggr's arm beside him.

But Tryggr clearly wasn't bothered, and if anything, he scented even stronger of triumph than before. And when Eben tentatively offered to wash up in the scullery, Tryggr scoffed and flatly refused, and ordered him to the Skai baths instead.

"I'm not having m'pet wash in a scullery," he snapped. "Skai-kesh knows you've already borne enough in here, ach? You're mine now, which means you're gonna get proper care, and a proper bath."

Eben flushed and shyly smiled, and allowed Tryggr to march him out through the kitchen, past an amused but unsurprised-looking Gegnir, and into the corridor. Where, Eben's fluttering thoughts soon realized, his state and his scent very clearly announced just how matters stood, to anyone who walked by. Including several former patients, a wide-eyed Ka-esh engineer, and—Eben's breath caught—*Gareth*.

And curse it, perhaps Gareth had come to check on the washing machines, but now he halted mid-step in the corridor, his eyes widening on Eben's face, and then flicking to his bruised, bitten neck. While beside Eben, Tryggr flashed Gareth a toothy, not-so-nice smile, and blatantly palmed at Eben's arse.

Eben could scent Gareth's surprise, followed by something much like jealousy—but then he made an obvious effort to smile, as he gave them a curt little nod. "I see I owe you my best wishes, brothers," he said, though his voice hitched. "If you ever have need of a *kraga*, only come to me, ach?"

Eben blinked, more heat flooding into his cheeks as he glanced sideways at Tryggr—who was still looking smug, and perhaps a little thoughtful, as he nodded back, and then ushered Eben past Gareth down the corridor. "Remind me, pet," he said, "what's a *kraga*? Not those pretty little gold collars you Ka-esh sometimes wear?"

Eben's steps faltered—Tryggr was asking about *kragas*?!—and a slow, dangerous grin was already pulling at Tryggr's mouth, his claws coming up to tickle at Eben's newly marked neck. "Ach, I see," he said, lower. "Would look real nice on you, pet, wouldn't it?"

Oh, hell, Eben truly could not breathe, amidst the shock and the abject yearning, and Tryggr kept smiling at him, dark and hungry, as his claws scraped a little harder. And it was so distracting that Eben didn't even notice when Tryggr guided him sideways into a room. Not the Skai baths, but—wait—the sickroom?

"Didn't bring you here to work, pet," Tryggr said quickly, with a reassuring smile toward him. "Just want to be sure you're well, ach?"

Oh. Tryggr had brought Eben here as—a patient. And even as Eben balked and waved it away, Kesst was already striding over to greet them, his arched brows rapidly rising. While across the room, Eben caught sight of Salvi, who must have just returned from his trip north—and who was now grinning at him with bright, jubilant glee.

"What's this?" Kesst asked, his voice sharp. "Good gods, you *reek* of Skai, Eben—and you haven't *injured* him, have you, Tryggr?"

"'Course not," Tryggr snapped back, even as his arm tightened possessively around Eben's shoulders. "Just finally settled things between us, and wanted to make sure he's looked after, and cared for. As he *should* be."

He'd fixed Kesst with a pointed frown, while across the room Efterar cleared his throat, and strode over to join them. "Thanks, Tryggr," he said firmly. "We've been learning we could use the help, right, Sweet-Fang?"

He'd gently elbowed Kesst in the side as he'd spoken, his gaze already focused on Eben's neck, his hand rising to hover over it. "And we're thankful for the Skai—and the Ka-esh— who offer their help so freely," he continued, "without demanding anything in return."

Wait. Was Efterar talking about Tryggr—and about Eben? But yes, Efterar's eyes darting toward Eben's face were grateful, and a little regretful, too. "I know I haven't said it enough," he added, "but you're an exceptional colleague, Eben. You've made yourself an expert in your field, you have an incredible work ethic, our patients love you—and you often see things the rest of us don't. It's a real help, and we're lucky to have you. Thanks."

Truly? Eben's face was smarting even hotter than before, his eyes prickling, his head rapidly shaking—but beside him, Tryggr gave a low harrumph, his arm squeezing tightly around Eben's shoulders. "Ach, you *are* lucky to have him," he said coolly. "And from now on, he's gonna be putting in less time here, too. He's gonna be moving in with me, and I'll be making sure he's got plenty of time to read, and fuck, and *sleep*."

Wait, he was?! But there wasn't the slightest hesitation in Tryggr's scent as he promptly wheeled Eben around, and marched him back toward the door. And when Eben gave a distracted wave goodbye over his shoulder, Efterar and Kesst both smiled and waved back, even though Eben heard Kesst mutter something about *obnoxious Skai fuckboys* under his breath. While at his workbench, Salvi was still gleefully grinning, and giving Eben a salute with his jar of tonic that clearly said, *I told you so.*

"Are you... sure, about that?" Eben managed, once Tryggr was ushering him down the corridor again. "Me... moving in with you?"

Tryggr's glance toward him was surprised, and a bit mulish, too. "Ach, yes," he said flatly. "I'm not moving down into that dank little hole of yours, and it seems to me you don't like it much, either. And you're mine now, so it's my job to keep a close eye on you, and take care of you."

His voice was clipped, decisive, though his eyes were searching Eben's now, as if seeking some kind of argument— but Eben's head was nodding, his breath exhaling, as a warm, settled relief shimmered up his spine. He didn't need to make a decision on this. He didn't need to agonize over what to tell his Ka-esh kin about why he was leaving. He could just... obey.

And he could obey in this, too. In Tryggr guiding him into the otherwise empty Skai bath—which was an admittedly impressive feat of Ka-esh engineering, with its frothy waterfall streaming out of the wall. And once Tryggr had stripped them both bare, tossing their clothes onto a nearby bench, he gripped Eben's arse, and guided him beneath the rush of ice-cold water.

"There we go, pet," Tryggr murmured, as he gently tugged out Eben's already-wet braid with his claws, and drew his hair back from his face. "Gonna clean you up real good now, aren't we?"

Eben could only nod and shiver, tilting his head back into that sweet scrape of Tryggr's claws. And then into the warm, dizzying touch of Tryggr's slippery, soapy hands, caressing all over his skin. Washing his neck, his shoulders, his arms, his torso, his legs—and oh, even his helpless, straining cock.

"Gotta get this nice and clean, pet," Tryggr said, waggling his eyebrows as he firmly stroked it up and down, staggering Eben on his feet. "Polish it up real pretty, ach?"

Oh, fuck, Eben was already babbling, begging, arching up as Tryggr reached his other soapy hand to grip his taut bollocks—and then he was shouting, shaking, as he sprayed out into the water in a sharp, steady stream. While Tryggr just kept stroking, petting, as a smug, wicked smile curled on his lips.

"Look at you, pet," he murmured. "Messing like that all over the Skai baths, while your lord's just tryna get you clean. I ken I oughta bend you over my knee for this, ach?"

Oh, hell, he didn't mean it, or did he—but his devious smile had pulled even higher, and he firmly grasped Eben's arse again, and guided him out of the water. Toward one of the benches lining the bath's stone walls, and in a swift movement, Tryggr sank down onto it, gripped Eben by the hips, and then hauled him face-down over his *lap.*

Fuck. Even Eben's most wondrous fantasies had never imagined this, his lord pinning his bare, shivering body over his lap in the public Skai baths. But it was happening, it was, and Tryggr's warm hand was giving his upraised arse a firm, approving caress.

"This is what you get, pet," he purred, "when you misbehave for your lord. You're gonna need to be taught a lesson, ach?"

Eben gasped and shuddered, his prick already straining

against Tryggr's thigh, and Tryggr huffed a low, triumphant laugh as he gave Eben's arse another firm little squeeze. And then that warm hand drew back, away, waiting, oh—and landed in a firm, ringing slap.

It rang through Eben like a jolt, like a surging shock of raging craving—and oh, the way Tryggr laughed again, easy and exultant, as Eben squirmed and moaned. As that hand began caressing his arse-cheek again, letting its claws sink in, before drawing back, and slapping again. And then again, and again, each strike making Eben shout and tremble, firing him deeper and deeper into the screeching, frantic frenzy.

"Good, pet," Tryggr breathed, between slaps, though Eben could taste his own reeling hunger now, too. "You're being such a good little thing, aren't you? Bearing your punishment so well. Letting your lord teach you a lesson."

Eben's moans lurched even higher, his body writhing in Tryggr's lap, and Tryggr's laugh was almost a groan this time. "Such a good pet, sweet thing," he gasped, as his hand lingered, caressed, before striking again. "So fucking good. Ach, I've wanted to do this since the first time I saw you, knew you'd be just the thing, just the sweetest, so pretty with your tight little arse up in the air, with my big red handprints all over it—"

Fuck, fuck, Eben was so close, he was about to blow, right here on Tryggr's lap—and he had to force himself to stillness, squeeze his eyes shut, bite his lip as hard as he could. And for an instant, he could taste Tryggr's confusion, his hand spasming against his arse—and then the scent of his comprehension, and another low, approving laugh.

"Ach, are you tryna keep from messing on me, sweet thing?" Tryggr asked, breathless. "Are you being a good little pet? Learning all your lessons?"

Eben desperately, fervently nodded, and Tryggr laughed again, his hand now caressing Eben's burning arse-cheeks.

"Good, pet," he murmured. "Even better than I thought. I ken you deserve a little treat from your lord, ach?"

Oh, yes, please, and Eben rapidly nodded again, and willingly allowed Tryggr's strong hands to grip him, and turn him over. So he was now lying face-up and naked over Tryggr's lap, his straining, dripping cock jutting straight upwards, for anyone to see...

And wait, anyone could see, oh hell. Because Eben hadn't even noticed that there were now a handful of Skai in the room, and they'd all been standing there, and watching Tryggr *spank* him. But Tryggr's eyes were only on him, only on Eben's hard, ruddy cock, and he inhaled slow and deep, his eyes fluttering, as he shifted Eben upwards on the bench, bent over him, and...

Sucked Eben into his *mouth.*

Eben shouted and arched, his eyes rolling back, because a Skai was sucking him, surrounding him with slick, hungry heat. Wanting him, rewarding him, giving his pet a treat, oh hell—and there was no way to control it, no way to keep it in, only breaking, spraying, surging it out into that tight, wonderful mouth. And Tryggr was swallowing it, drinking it up with all apparent eagerness, sucking out every last drop, until Eben was shaky and spent all over.

"Fuck," he gasped, without at all meaning to, as his body arched into a hard, aching shudder. "Th-thank you, sir."

He only vaguely heard the low, approving chuckles from the other Skai now in the room, because there was only Tryggr, drawing up and licking his lips, as hunger crackled and shimmered in his scent. "You deserved it, pet," he murmured. "An' you taste just as sweet as you look, ach?"

Eben couldn't even speak, not beneath the awe and the ache and the fervour, and suddenly it was all too much, too impossibly overwhelming, shivering all through his body, prickling behind his eyes. And maybe Tryggr saw it, or even understood it, his warm hands stroking Eben, caressing him, reassuring him. And then gripping him again, and this time, moving him... downwards. Down so he was kneeling between Tryggr's thighs on the hard floor, with—oh—Tryggr's scarred, swollen cock jutting straight toward his mouth.

"In your mouth, pet," Tryggr breathed, his claws sinking into Eben's hair. "An' I don't want you even *thinking* about making it good for me, ach? You just relax, and drink. As much as you want."

Oh. Oh, he wasn't offering that, but he was, he was. His strong hand now drawing Eben's head forward, filling Eben's mouth with his waiting, dripping prick. With that wondrous rich sweet taste of him, and when Eben drew down a tentative swallow, Tryggr smiled softly toward him, and sank his other hand into Eben's hair, too.

"Good, pet," he murmured. "Just like that. An' you can bite it too, if you want."

Wait. Wait, truly? Eben could—*do* that? But yes, oh, Tryggr's smile had gone a bit bemused, his hands stroking deeper through Eben's hair. "Anytime you want, sweet thing," he continued, softer. "Gotta feed my pretty pet properly, you ken."

Eben couldn't hide his moan, or his brash, furious longing, his teeth already settling tentative against the tender skin of Tryggr's shaft in his mouth. But Tryggr just kept watching, smiling, stroking, waiting—so Eben gathered his courage, and bit down into that hard, pulsing flesh.

The blood instantly swarmed into his mouth, blending heady and rich with the sweet seeping seed—and *fuck*, it was good, so good, maybe the best thing Eben had ever tasted in all his days. And he was already moaning, sucking harder, even as he darted a pleading, apologetic look up at Tryggr's face—but Tryggr was still just smiling at him, fond and approving, as the hunger flashed higher in his scent, and a distinctive flush stained his cheeks.

"Ach, just thus, pet," he said, hoarse. "Just what you've been needing, I ken."

Oh, this couldn't be happening, Eben had never known anything like this, had never needed anything like this. His lord so freely feeding him the most priceless, most precious meal in all the realm, while still caressing him, smiling at him, approving of him. And when another Skai strode over, and signed something at Tryggr, Eben didn't mind in the slightest—and it might have been even more contented, wonderful warmth, pooling in his belly. Tryggr didn't care who saw this. Tryggr maybe even wanted his clanmates to see this, his sweet Ka-esh pet kneeling between his sprawled thighs, and suckling out his good Skai sustenance.

"No, I'm not sharing him," Tryggr told the new orc, though his voice was mild, even smug. "You can go get your own, just like I did. An' also"—he hesitated, his eyes gone thoughtful on the orc's face, even as he kept caressing Eben's head—"you ken, there are some sweet Ka-esh down there who'd make you fight 'em for it. An' even whip you with this vicious lash they got, too."

That seemed... specific, and Eben's hazy eyes darted sideways, fought to focus on the new orc's face. And wait, damn it, it was that same handsome Skai Tryggr had been fucking in the corridor, that very first day Eben had seen him—and the orc's expression was one of mingled disappointment and curiosity, his eyes lingering on Eben's face.

And oh, Tryggr was drawing Eben's face forward, now, sinking himself a bit deeper—showing Eben off for this orc, oh hell. "Pretty, though, ain't he?" Tryggr said, with distinct satisfaction. "Damned good with his mouth, too. Can even suck me full down his tight little throat, can't you, pretty pet?"

Oh, yes, yes, Eben could, and did Tryggr mean he wanted to

show them—and yes, he did, and Eben wanted to show them, too. Because there were more Skai, coming over to see, to watch, and Eben drew in a breath, held his eyes on Tryggr's face, and slowly, surely, sucked him deep. Burying that huge Skai cock down his opened, spasming throat, and then holding it there, sucking as hard as he could, while Tryggr watched with hungry, fluttering eyes, his hands skittering in Eben's hair.

"So good, pet," Tryggr crooned, husky and hot, as his cock swelled even fuller in Eben's mouth. "So sweet. An' you're gonna be even sweeter once you're stuffed full of Skai seed, ach? Once you're reeking of me from both ends, just like the perfect little pet you are?"

Yes, please, *please*, Eben's groan burning through his convulsing, blocked-off throat, his tongue frantically caressing the hard flesh cramming into his mouth, his wide eyes pleading on Tryggr's face—and oh, the way Tryggr shouted and bent double as he sprayed out, blasting surge after surge of fresh Skai seed straight down into Eben's open, spasming throat.

One of the watching orcs whistled, low and approving, but Eben's full focus was still on caressing Tryggr's convulsing prick, milking out every bit of that sweet Skai seed, while holding his eyes to Tryggr's flushed face. Needing his praise, his approval, and yes, it was already here, Tryggr's shaky hands stroking his hot cheeks, his hair, his bulging throat.

"So pretty, Ka-esh," he choked. "So sweet. So perfect. *Ach*."

And it was perfect, it was, Tryggr flaunting Eben, praising Eben, touching him, filling him. Flooding him with his scent and his pleasure, to the point where Eben could scarcely see the others, couldn't even make out their scents, so perfect and safe and content...

At least, until his hazy, blinking eyes caught a glimpse of a huge, hulking orc, striding into the room—and Eben froze, jolted backwards, as distant recognition spiked through his thoughts, tangled with vivid, horrible memories of that day in the arena. Of himself, exposed, compromised, weak, as that—this?—Skaap orc had trapped him, threatened him, wanted to—

"Ach, Ka-esh!" Tryggr yelped, as strong hands hauled Eben up, clutched him tight and close into his lap. "Ach, don't scent thus! Naught to fear! You're safe, pet. *Safe.*"

Oh. Eben was still shivering, clinging to Tryggr, as his bleary eyes finally focused on the orc at the door, and found—Ulfarr. Oh, curse it, it was only Ulfarr, foolish, foolish, what would they think of him, what would Tryggr think of him—

"S-sorry," he gulped, too quickly, into Tryggr's chest. "F-foolish. Just thought it was—someone else."

Tryggr's firm hands were still gripping him, caressing him, but there was no judgement in his scent. Only a sudden, grim comprehension as his breath huffed out, and his hands drew Eben even closer than before.

"Ach, I see," he said quiet. "But naught to fear, pet, for Skaap is dead."

Wait. Skaap was—dead?! And Eben jolted again, staring at Tryggr's face, as yet more alarm roiled through his chest. He hadn't wanted to cause any trouble, let alone an orc's *death*, and had it been his fault, his doing, no, no, no—

"I ken it's distressing, pet, but it had to be done," Tryggr said, his voice a little harder, his hands still stroking firmly at Eben's skin. "Turned out you weren't the only one—or even the only Ka-esh—Skaap forced to his bidding. An' he had plenty of chances to make amends, but instead he spoke false to us and kept at it, ach? Couldn't let it go any further, pet. Need to keep kin like you *safe.*"

Oh. Eben was slightly relaxing again, though he couldn't help an uneasy glance around at the other watching Skai, too. Expecting, perhaps, some kind of resistance, or judgement—

but there was only the same grim, flinty certainty, and even a few curt nods.

"We ken you Ka-esh have oft feared us, pet," Tryggr said, soft again. "But we don't wish you to run and hide from us, as you so oft do, ach? Wish you to trust us, and know we'll do our jobs, and keep you safe. Whilst we trust you to keep our mountain standing, give us safe air, offer us help and medicine, and all the other good you do for us. So much good, Ka-esh."

There was genuine emotion in his voice, in his hand's all-encompassing wave at the room, the mountain, at Eben himself. And as Eben blinked back, the last of his father's words seemed to whisper away, vanishing into the steady splash of the bath's pouring water. *Never trust a... let one find you...*

Eben swallowed hard, gave a faint little sniffle, twitched a shaky, grateful smile at Tryggr's face. And Tryggr was smiling back, looking distinctly relieved, as warmth and affection shimmered in his eyes. "Good, Ka-esh," he murmured. "So it had naught to do with you, and you don't need to spare it another thought, ach? An' if it helps at all"—he darted a glance upwards—"I ken Skaap's death was quick and easy, too. Ach, brother?"

And wait, he was talking to Ulfarr, whose huge, stiff body was still standing near the door, his hands in tight fists at his sides. But then he nodded, curt and decisive, even as something like regret, or maybe grief, glinted in his eyes.

"Ach, it was kinder than he deserved," he said, his voice hard. "We are most sorry, Ka-esh, for the fear and pain he brought you. Henceforth, we shall do our utmost to keep you safe."

He accompanied the words with a bow of his head, a clutch of his big fist over his heart. And Eben's own heart skipped a beat, his body relaxing heavier into Tryggr's, his head twitching a nod. "Th-thank you," he whispered. "That is—very kind."

Ulfarr grimaced, but then nodded, and headed for the door. At least, until he hesitated and glanced back toward Tryggr, signing something Eben couldn't fully follow. Something about—vexed fathers?

"Ach, Skai-kesh above," Tryggr muttered, as he rolled his eyes, and ran a hand against his still-wet hair, now half-fallen out of his topknot. "Shoulda known he'd be scenting, and prowling about in high dudgeon."

Eben's body sat up straight again, his eyes searching uneasily at Tryggr's face. But Tryggr flashed him a wry, reassuring grin, and clapped a steady hand to his shoulder. Safe. *Safe.*

"C'mon, pet," he said firmly. "And let's go meet your new kin."

22

Tryggr wanted to introduce Eben to his new kin.

Those unexpected, unnerving words simmered low in Eben's belly as Tryggr promptly drew him to his feet again, tossed him his trousers, and began combing out his hair with his claws. "So pretty, Ka-esh," he murmured. "Mind if I leave this down, for now?"

Eben didn't mind, of course, and he was soon treated to the sight of Tryggr with his own long hair down, too. The dark shiny fall of it beautifully framing his handsome face, setting off his warm eyes, and Tryggr dragged his fingers through it with far more force than he'd used on Eben, his dagger glinting silver in his teeth. And Eben blinked as he watched, heat pooling in his belly, before he belatedly reached a shaky hand for the dagger, and plucked it out of Tryggr's mouth.

"This could break your teeth, sir," he said, though his face was already burning. "Or cut your mouth, also."

But if Tryggr was bothered at being corrected by his pet, he didn't at all show it, and instead winked at Eben, and reached to swipe a finger down the blade's gleaming edge. "Ain't sharp thus, pet," he said. "Only the tip, ach? Don't want a haircut every time I put it up, you ken. But"—he leaned down and pressed a brief kiss to Eben's forehead—"thanks for looking out for me, sweet thing."

Eben's face flushed even hotter, and he watched with awed fascination as Tryggr deftly wound his wet hair around the dagger, and then twisted it, stabbing it into place. "Ready, then, pet?" he said lightly, though there was a distinct carefulness in his scent, too. "Pa's likely spitting knives out there waiting, I ken."

Well, that was disconcerting, but Tryggr's solid hand was again grasping Eben's arse, and guiding him toward the door. Toward where—yes—there were two orcs waiting outside, both of them staring at Tryggr and Eben with blatant curiosity. One of the orcs was scarred and bulky, and vaguely familiar— Eben's distant thoughts rapidly placed him as a former patient—while the other, taller and leaner with a dagger in his silver topknot, was entirely new. Except for the distinct flavour in his scent, which was very much like Tryggr's.

"Leave it to you, Pa," Tryggr said to the silver-haired orc, with an aggrieved roll of his eyes toward the bulky one. "Couldn't even let us get a damned bath in, ach?"

But Tryggr's father only pulled himself up taller, frowning down his nose at his son. "What's this I'm hearing about you and this Ka-esh, son?" he demanded, with a brief, searching glance toward Eben. "Heard you've been going around calling him your *pet*?"

Eben couldn't hide the sudden alarm in his scent, his body angling slightly backwards—but Tryggr held him firm and close, even as his other hand signed something toward his father that might have been, *Watch it, Pa.*

"Ach, Pa, this is Eben, of Clan Ka-esh," Tryggr said, voice clipped. "He's a brilliant medic and researcher, and the sweetest, bravest thing I've ever met in my life. So ach, we've decided he's gonna be my new pet. An' Eben"—Tryggr waved between his father and the bulky orc—"this is Pa, and *Pabbi*."

For an instant, both orcs stared between Tryggr and Eben, with stunned disbelief in their eyes and scents. Until Tryggr's *pabbi* twitched a little shake, and then gave Eben a warm smile, and a swift bow. "Greetings, Eben," he said in a soft, pleasing voice. "I am Ezog, of Clan Bautul. I well recall your great kindness in the sickroom when I was last wounded, ach? And this"—his gaze flicked sideways—"is Sigtryggr, most oft called Tryg."

Eben attempted a polite smile between them both, though his rapidly whirling brain had noted that Ezog hadn't actually explained his relationship to Tryg, despite the impressive depth of their scents upon one another. Suggesting that they'd been intimate for many years, but even so, Tryg's scent—and only Tryg's scent—also spoke distinctly of a *woman*. And suddenly Tryggr's comment about what he'd witnessed with his pa and *pabbi* made even more sense than before, because Tryg was bedding both a woman, *and* this Ezog, while Ezog's scent only spoke of Tryg.

It suggested at least some degree of inequality in the relationship, or perhaps even some unpleasantness on Tryg's part. And Eben felt himself drawing back a little further, his eyes uneasy on Tryg's face—and perhaps Tryg had caught it, his own eyes softening, his clawed hand running against his bound-back hair.

"Ach, well, it's good to finally meet you, Ka-esh," Tryg firmly told him, in a voice and accent that was deeply reminiscent of Tryggr's. "I've oft asked after your scent upon m'boy, but he kept giving me the runaround! Saying you were just a friend, and naught more!"

He cast a brief, accusing glance toward Tryggr, who was now frowning straight back. "Ach, you aren't the only one who can keep a secret, Pa," he snapped. "An' Eben was a friend, he *is*—but the more I kept an eye on him, the more I wanted to keep him, for good. An' I wanted to sort it out for myself, without having *you* poking your big nose in over it! Telling me I oughta be settling down with a woman, or a Skai, or some other such rubbish! You ken I've given it all a go, but none of it's struck me like Eben, and I'm not changing my mind!"

Eben's unease was now tangling with stunned, shimmering warmth—Tryggr really meant all that?—and he was distantly relieved when Ezog loudly cleared his throat, and elbowed Tryg in the side. "We are most pleased for you, son," Ezog told Tryggr, his voice firm. "And most glad to meet you, Eben. I am sure you shall be very happy together."

Oh. Tryggr shot Ezog a brief, grateful grin, followed by a pointed glance at his father—who was also twitching a wry, resigned smile, and clasping Tryggr on the shoulder. "Ach, we wish you well with him, son," he said. "An' he's a sweet little thing too, ain't he? Prettiest Ka-esh I've ever seen, I ken."

Tryggr looked somewhat mollified by this, drawing Eben closer into his side. "Ach, he is," he said firmly. "An' the cleverest, and bravest, and a right dream to fuck, too. Gonna make me a real good pet, I ken."

Well. Eben's face was burning again, ducking into Tryggr's shoulder, but he could taste Tryggr's satisfaction, his hand gripping possessively at his arse. And that hand was now steering Eben away, guiding him up the corridor again, without so much as a farewell to his pa and *pabbi* behind him.

"Leave it to Pa," Tryggr said irritably, once they were out of earshot. "Getting all uppity about me mating a Ka-esh, when he's never even bothered speaking vows to *Pabbi*! Never mind fucking around with that secret new woman of his, too!"

Wait. Wait, Eben had only followed half of that, because— had Tryggr just said—*mating* a Ka-esh? *Mating*? Swearing vows to one another? *Permanently*?

But yes, wait, Tryggr was hesitating, angling Eben a

searching, sidelong look. "Ach, well, if you'd want it, I mean," he said, a little rushed. "Just—it's not a small thing, for a Skai to take a pet, ach? An' a mate don't seem much different, does it?"

Eben couldn't even speak, just blinking helplessly at Tryggr here in the corridor, as wetness spilled from his eyes, and streaked down his cheeks. It couldn't be true, he couldn't mean it, he couldn't—but oh, Tryggr was rapidly blinking too, lurching toward Eben, wiping his thumbs against Eben's wet cheeks. "Ach, don't weep, pet," he murmured, husky, as he leaned forward, pressed a gentle kiss to Eben's forehead. "Wanna make you happy, ach?"

But Eben was, he was, he'd never been so happy in all his life, and he was frantically, fervently nodding. "You do, Tryggr," he gulped, between laughs, or maybe sobs. "You make me so happy. You were so generous, you showed me so much, you helped me when you did not need to, you were just—just—"

He couldn't even say it, there was no way to possibly describe it—and oh, oh, that was Tryggr's mouth, Tryggr's lips, finding Eben's own. Kissing him, tasting his mouth, for the very first time, please—and Eben moaned, desperate, helpless, as he kissed Tryggr back. Let his tongue seek and tangle, revelling in the lingering truth of his own seed on Tryggr's tongue—and then the scrape of sharp Skai teeth, and the taste of his own blood, too. All of it whirling together into a sweet, dizzying stream, and Tryggr was caught in it too, his own groan vibrating into Eben, his hands suddenly clawing at Eben's trousers, yanking them down, spinning Eben away, pressing him hard against the wall.

And this wasn't happening, it couldn't be happening, Eben's thoughts flashing back to that very first time he'd seen Tryggr. When he'd had that other orc bent over in this very corridor, caressing him, feeding his strong scarred prick up inside him, just—just—like this.

"Good, pet," Tryggr gasped, as that hard flesh fully

breached him, and began sinking inside. "Fuck, that's so good. So tight. *Ach.*"

Eben wildly nodded and shivered, squeezing as hard as he could, grinding back onto that sweet, stunning certainty. His Skai, his orc, maybe even his mate, breaking the rules, fucking him in a corridor, where anyone might see...

But in contrast to that first time Eben had seen him, Tryggr was leaning in close, and again... kissing him. His warm lips sweetly skating down Eben's neck, his collarbone, as his hand slipped around, and grasped Eben's hard, straining cock. Stroking him, caressing him, in time with his gentle thrusts inside. Holding him there, making Eben his, flaring him full of impossible happiness, rewriting that first moment they'd met. *I can show you the way.*

"So good," Tryggr gasped, grinding harder, his lips quivering on Eben's skin. "So sweet, pet. So perfect, so pretty, *mine—*"

And oh, oh, there it was, Eben's own release spraying all over the stone wall before him, furling him full of flaring, flying relief, while more of that sweet Skai seed surged deep inside. Flooding Eben from the bottom up, filling all his empty places, almost as if it had reached—he huffed a shivery little laugh— his heart.

"So good," Tryggr murmured again, hoarse, as his kisses kept pressing so sweetly against his skin. "Ach, sweet thing?"

"Ach," Eben whispered, soft and shimmering in his breath, his heart. "Perfect."

The first time Tryggr used the whip, Eben was bent over and begging in the Ka-esh *dýflissa*, with Tryggr buried bollocks-deep in his arse.

"More," Eben gasped, dragging his claws against the wall before him, lost in the pleasure and the frenzy, the stark desperate craving. "Give me more, sir. Please."

Behind him, Tryggr huffed a low, satisfied laugh, and gave a firm slap to Eben's trembling arse. "Ungrateful little pet," he drawled, as he slowly, deliberately drew backwards, falling free of Eben's grip with a jolting little squelch. "So damned greedy. After I spent all this past fortnight taking this pretty little arse to that library!"

He punctuated the words with another ringing slap to Eben's upraised rump, and Eben moaned and nodded, arching back toward Tryggr, opening up as wide as he could. Tempting his lord with a blatant view of what was on offer, showing his lord how pretty he was, how ready, how obedient...

"But it was so *good*, sir," he whimpered, as the visions of their trip north flashed up into his scattering thoughts. All those wonderful nights and days alone with Tryggr, walking and talking and fucking and laughing together, curling up together each night in dark quiet places underground. And finally, visiting the library itself—Osada's huge, wondrous provincial library, which had a covert agreement with the local Ka-esh, allowing private visits after nightfall in exchange for hand-transcribed copies of valuable ancient orc texts.

Eben's five nights at the library had quite possibly been the most mentally stimulating of his life, lost amidst mountains of books and notes, his thoughts bursting with new ideas and hypotheses and revelations. And also bursting with Tryggr, always Tryggr, who'd stayed with him, and fed him, and fucked him, and hadn't once spoken aloud the sheer boredom Eben had known he'd felt.

"*You* were so good," Eben gasped, still arching himself back as far as he could go, shivering at the feel of Tryggr's hot fresh seed spilling from him, streaking down his thighs. "You were the most generous—the most powerful—the most *magnificent* lord, and I only—*need* you, sir. Need you fucking me, wanting me, using me. Making me scream on your perfect Skai prick."

His voice was shaking by the end, his arse trembling, too, waiting, *please*. And fuck, yes, that was Tryggr's slick cock again, just teasing at Eben's open heat, as his hand gently scraped its claws down Eben's sweaty, shivering flank. "So greedy, sweet Ka-esh," Tryggr hissed, the triumph hot and low on his voice, in his scent. "Such a shameless little slag for Skai prick, aren't you? Never happy, unless this tight little hole's jammed full of it."

Eben fervently nodded, shoving back further, needing more, more, please. "Just yours," he choked out. "Just yours, sir. *Please.*"

But oh, Tryggr was taking his time, making it last, his hand now clutching tight to Eben's hip, holding him in place. "Thing is, pretty Ka-esh," Tryggr drawled, "a good lord can't let his favourite pet get spoilt, ach? Can't just reward your selfish greed thus, you ken. Gotta teach you a few lessons first."

Oh, yes, please, Eben's moan escaped all on its own, his arse shoving back harder, as his head jerked another frantic nod. And behind him Tryggr laughed again, bright and smug and indulgent—and then he leaned forward, so his hand could pluck something from the wall beside Eben. The short coiled *whip.*

Wait. *Wait.* Eben froze all over, his head snapping around to stare at Tryggr's face. At where his cheeks were deeply flushed, his eyes hooded, his tongue slipping against his lips. "But only if you want, Eben," he said, softer, hoarse. "If you're sure, about what you told me."

Eben's stunned, frantic thoughts instantly jolted backwards, back to one of those nights on their trip, when a laughing Tryggr had begun teasingly swatting at Eben's bare arse with a switch—and then he'd stopped, wincing, shaking his head. *Sorry, Eben,* he'd said. *Swore we wouldn't use lashes. Don't wanna play into you needing it. Making the pain real with it.*

Eben had flinched at the words, and he'd had to fight back the reflexive, rising urge to babble some stupid excuse, to turn and run, to find a cave and curl up and weep. Because that had been real concern in Tryggr's searching eyes, maybe even real fear. And whenever Tryggr used Eben's name like this, it meant they weren't playing anymore. It meant he wanted Eben's truth, and his heart. And Tryggr had been such a good lord to Eben, such a good friend, and he deserved Eben's answer. His honesty.

I ken I did—use it that way, Eben had finally replied, between heavy breaths. *Too much. But since we—since I—have begun to face this pain in other ways, I—I ken I do not now need it, thus. But I yet would—welcome this, from you. Very much. The pain with the pleasure, it is just—just—*

He hadn't been able to continue, his face burning, his eyes

wide and fearful on Tryggr's face. But his cock had been brazenly straining and leaking, his hunger and longing choking his breath. And finally, Tryggr had flashed him a wry, crooked little smile, and given his arse a gentle slap with the switch.

Ach, then, he'd said. *We'll try it. But if I scent any of that on you, we're stopping. And I need you to be honest with me over it, too. Need to be able to trust you.*

But Eben knew how Tryggr felt about honesty, knew how much it meant to him, and he'd rapidly nodded, his hand over his heart. *I promise, Tryggr*, he'd said. *And—thank you.*

It had led to a truly glorious evening, full of teasing taunts and swats from Tryggr's switch, until Eben had been spread-eagled and babbling and begging, and had emptied his bollocks no fewer than three separate times. And afterwards, he hadn't missed the surprising depth of the satisfaction in Tryggr's scent, or the way his fingers had gently traced over the marks he'd left in Eben's skin.

Look what you did, pet, he'd murmured. *Letting a Skai rough you up like this. Letting him leave all these pretty new marks all over you.*

It had been perfect, perfect, and they'd done more of it in the nights afterwards, until Tryggr had drawn Eben's blood with it, and then carefully licked and healed his wounds. And that had been perfect too, a strange, shivering wonder unlike anything Eben had ever known, ever tasted. But he'd still never imagined Tryggr would end up changing his mind about the whip—let alone here in the *dýflissa*, where Eben had so often misused the pain in the past.

But Tryggr was still holding the whip, still watching Eben with his brows raised, and Eben shuddered all over, swallowed down the catch in his throat. "Yes," he gulped. "Yes, Tryggr, please. It would—mean so much to me. Most of all—here."

He cast a brief, sweeping glance around at the familiar dark room, his familiar clanmates, most of them focused on taking their joy together, but a few of them curiously watching this, too. Wanting to see a Skai wielding a Ka-esh whip, perhaps. Wanting to see a Skai embracing the ways of the Ka-esh clan, and the well-known, long-term preferences of his Ka-esh lover.

Tryggr briefly followed Eben's glance, his breath exhaling, and he twitched a curt little nod. "Good, pet," he murmured, quiet. "An' you're gonna be good for me, aren't you? You're gonna tell me if it's too much, or I'm fucking it up?"

There was a genuine flicker of unease in his eyes, or even nervousness, but Eben was already nodding, his eyes wide and warm and worshipful. And then he turned back to face the wall again, his body shivering as it arched, as he felt more hot seed spilling down his arse, and leaking from his own swollen, straining cock.

"Please, sir," he gasped. "Please, teach me a lesson. Make me learn to behave for you. Make me a good little pet for you, make me scream and beg for you, *please*."

Tryggr's gasp was low and harsh, and fuck, that was the cool leather fall of the whip, trailing slow and taunting against Eben's back. The sensation so familiar, so shockingly powerful, and Eben quivered all over at even this, at the threat of it, the promise of it. At how Tryggr's hard, leaking prick was gently nudging into him, now, opening him up, as that leather tickled and teased, trailed all over Eben's skin. As if Tryggr somehow already knew how to use it, but of course he did, Skai trained with all manner of weapons, and it was already so, so good...

"Please, sir," Eben croaked as he clamped tight at that hot hard flesh, sought to shove back further. "Please, plough me. Punish me. Make your pet spurt and scream for you. *Please*."

And yes, yes, Tryggr's breath hitching, the lash finally drawing back—and with a hiss and a sting, the pain flashed across Eben's back, and Tryggr's huge, powerful prick plunged sharp and deep into his arse.

Eben's shout echoed through the room, his head snapping back, his legs quaking—and fuck, fuck, Tryggr was holding himself there, waiting, grinding hard, as the lash trailed light against Eben's prickling skin. "You learning yet, pet?" he asked, and oh, that was the feel of Tryggr bending low so he could scent at Eben's neck, his breath inhaling deep. "You learning how to behave for your Skai?"

Eben pressed up as hard as he could, clamped Tryggr's cock as tight as he could, and wildly shook his head. "No," he gasped. "I need more. *More.*"

And oh, the way Tryggr's laugh rumbled into him, those familiar teeth gently nipping at his sweaty throat. "Greedy little pet," he murmured, as he stood up again, gave a swat of his free hand to Eben's arse. "Such a selfish, stubborn little slag for Skai prick. You're gonna get what you deserve, aren't you?"

Eben's moans were rising, his head nodding, as Tryggr laughed again, hot and triumphant—and then the whip licked back, as his cock drew out, taunting, waiting, wanting...

And then it all slammed Eben at once, Tryggr's driving cock, the swinging stinging whip. Spattering out pain and pleasure, smashing them into a single screeching stream of bright, vivid ecstasy—and then again, and again, and again. Tryggr's cock slamming into him, Tryggr's whip striking across his back, Tryggr's claws biting into the skin of his hip. So much, so raw, so perfect, so starkly, staggeringly powerful that Eben could only shout and submit, open up wide to the brutal blistering beauty, to the sweet stabbing surrender. To the impossible wonder of his Skai, his mate, using him, punishing him, ploughing him, breaking him.

And fuck, Tryggr was already close, already there, hissing a hoarse, desperate cry as he plunged strong and deep—and then hot spurts of Skai seed surged out of him, flooding fast and fierce into Eben, filling him full...

"Empty yourself for me, pet," came Tryggr's order, harsh

and ragged behind him, as his clawed hand slipped around to grip at Eben's own straining cock, pumping up once, twice. "Behave, and obey your Skai lord. *Now*."

And Eben couldn't control it, couldn't withstand it, could only stagger and scream as his own aching, throbbing prick finally, finally erupted. Spewing out so hard it hurt, streaming with not only his seed, but with—other liquid, too. With *everything*.

The scent of it was pungent and shameful in Eben's desperate breaths, but oh he couldn't stop, he couldn't, he was lost, caught, his entire body shuddering as his prick kept spouting, emptying, obeying. On and on and on, pouring out all that Tryggr asked, because Tryggr had done this, how the hell had Tryggr done this, and what if—what if—

And Tryggr was watching it, oh, grinding and caressing him through it, his breath inhaling against Eben's neck, his claws dragging gently down his sides. Waiting until Eben's helpless, frenzied spraying had finally subsided into sputtering little spasms, and his quaking body sagged against the wall, utterly empty, utterly spent.

"*Fuck*, pet," Tryggr groaned, husky into Eben's neck. "Ach, you're so good. So tight. So sweet. So perfect. *Ach*."

Eben was still shivering all over, his face flooded with heat, his mortified eyes darting downwards to where—his breath heaved out—all the evidence of his humiliation had at least vanished down the grate that lined the wall, meant for just such purposes. But surely Tryggr had smelled it, his breath still drawing in deep, his lips kissing at Eben's neck.

"So perfect, pet," he repeated, softer than before. "Such a good, clever little thing, aren't you? Learning how to open up and obey for your Skai, just like a good pet should. An' I bet"— his voice hitched lower—"none of these other pricks ever made you mess yourself like this for them, did they? Even when they used this lash on you?"

Eben furiously shook his head, the shame still burning in his cheeks, and Tryggr's laugh was low and hot, simmering with a rather vicious-sounding triumph. "Good," he murmured. "An' no need to scent thus, pet. Any good lord knows his pet's bound to make a little mess now an' then, ach? 'Specially with a strong Skai prick fucking it outta him."

Oh. More triumph had flared into Tryggr's scent, into his hungry, smoky voice, and oh, it meant—he'd *liked* it. He'd liked having that power, liked making Eben do something no one else had ever done, especially here, in this room where Eben had found pleasure with so many other orcs.

It was enough to soften Eben's body again, to slightly slow his rapid breaths, and yes, Tryggr was purring his approval, gently kissing at his throat. And then drawing himself out of Eben with a soft squelch, so he could ease his mouth downwards. Licking with careful, focused attention on the welts and wounds the whip had made, working over each one until Eben could feel that familiar prickle of healing, as the lingering pain drifted further and further away. And fuck, now Tryggr had even slipped down to Eben's crease, blatantly swirling his clever tongue into Eben's tender hole. Making it open up around him, oh, releasing a surge of his own hot seed into his mouth...

But Tryggr had never minded such things, and that might have been even more triumph on his scent as he kept licking, tending, swallowing. Scattering Eben with more warmth and wonder and pleasure, until he was fully hard again, and desperately grinding back into that slick, wicked mouth. To which Tryggr only laughed, the feel of it shivering into Eben's very core, as his warm clawed hand came around to grasp Eben, and began pumping him with slow, lazy strokes. Swarming him with yet more thrilling, impossible bliss, until he was staggering and shouting again, his cock sputtering out the last paltry dregs of his seed into the drain at his feet.

Afterwards it was only pleasure again, soft and hazy and sweet, and Tryggr gently drew Eben up, turned him around, pressed his back into the wall. And then Tryggr blocked him in, keeping him there, as his mouth kissed down Eben's forehead, his cheek, his throat. Until he found his favourite place, just in the crook of Eben's shoulder, and Eben willingly arched for it, welcoming it, as Tryggr's sharp teeth sank deep. His swallows already gulping, loud and rapid and eager, while Eben's trembling hands stroked Tryggr's back, smoothing steady and firm over his sweaty skin. Feeling how his wiry, familiar body slowly softened beneath the touch, sagging heavier and heavier against Eben, as a deep, palpable relief shivered through his scent.

That relief was something that had taken Eben a while to notice and understand these past months, and something he'd begun to treasure, too. Like so many of his fellow Skai, Tryggr seemed perpetually compelled to show only strength, to assume and project power, to prove he could please and protect those he cared about. It was a mentality that had seemed to permeate the entire clan, and even Tryggr's cheerful, well-meaning pa had instilled it deep into his son, insisting that he do more, prove more, work more, give more to keep their kin safe, and rebuild their clan.

But after having borne such similar weight so long himself—and having experienced Tryggr's help in releasing it—Eben had begun doing all within his power to give Tryggr relief from it, too. Encouraging him to take breaks from scouting and training, asking him to rest when he was injured, bringing him sweets and treats and tonics whenever he could. Offering up not only his knowledge in such matters, but his affection, his reassurance, his pleasure, his care. Being the place Tryggr could always come to, the place Tryggr could always trust, the place Tryggr could be weak or vulnerable or painfully honest. The place where Tryggr was always, always safe, always valued and welcomed and cherished, just the way he was.

And Eben could taste it now, that sweet, soft contentment in Tryggr's scent, the languid ease in his lean body beneath Eben's steady stroking touch. The way his hungry swallows had slowed, his breath heavily sighing, until he gently drew out his teeth, and began licking at where he'd bitten. But not fully healing it, not all the way, because he liked seeing his teeth-marks on Eben's neck, and Eben loved seeing them, too.

"Thanks, sweet thing," Tryggr finally murmured, on another slow, shuddering exhale. "So fucking good."

Eben nodded and huffed a shaky laugh, his hands still stroking Tryggr's back. "Ach, it was," he whispered. "I loved this so much, Tryggr. I love *you*."

He could hear Tryggr's hard swallow, the brief hitch of his breath. "You—you too, Eben," he whispered back. "An' ach, you ken, I—I got something for you. If you wanna come see?"

His voice sounded strangely tentative, almost nervous, enough that Eben twitched back, searching his face—but Tryggr was already turning away, swiping up their clothes from the nearby bench. So Eben rapidly nodded and dressed, and then followed Tryggr out into the corridor. To where Tryggr wasn't leading him back up toward the rest of the mountain, toward their work or their room. But instead, he was taking Eben to...

The Ka-esh *forge?*

Eben blinked at Tryggr, frowning, but Tryggr's eyes stayed intent on the forge as he firmly ushered Eben inside. It was as hot and bright as always, the rhythmic clangs of the smiths' pounding ringing through the smoke-scented air. And of course, one of the smiths was Gareth, and across the room, he'd already lifted his visor and waved them over with an eager sweep of his hand.

Eben went, feeling more mystified by the moment,

especially when Gareth led them into the forge's back room, where the smiths' work was displayed for viewing and purchase. "Over here, brothers," he said, as he gestured at a small shelf, covered with glittering gold items. "I finished it just yesterday, ach? You shall be pleased, I ken."

Eben was fully frowning now, blinking blankly between Gareth and Tryggr, and that was more nervousness on Tryggr's scent, in his eyes, as he briefly pulled Gareth close, and clapped his hand to his shoulder. "Thanks, brother," he said, a little thick. "This was real good of you."

Gareth's smile was both surprised and pleased, and he firmly clapped Tryggr back. "It was an honour," he replied. "I am glad to have held your trust in such an important matter."

Gareth's warm eyes flicked to Eben, who was feeling entirely lost, now—and finally Tryggr nodded, and cleared his throat. And then he reached an unsteady hand to pluck up a glittering item from the nearby shelf, and it was—

A *kraga*.

Eben's heart thudded, his body struck to sharp, sudden stillness. No. *No*. Tryggr hadn't made him a *kraga*. He couldn't. He wouldn't. And yes, maybe Tryggr had continued to make a few offhanded comments about *kragas* now and then, but Eben had never allowed himself to believe it. Not even after they'd sworn the vows of matehood to one another, and Tryggr had then fucked him over and over again in the Skai common-room, while all his clan bore witness...

But—a *kraga*. An unbreakable, permanent ring of Ka-esh gold, meant to be worn until death. A *kraga*.

Water had begun prickling behind Eben's eyes, and it felt too hard to breathe, to look away from the *kraga* in Tryggr's fingers, as the waves of shock and longing kept raging up and down his spine. A *kraga*. From *Tryggr*. For *him*.

"Ach, your scent, pet," came Tryggr's soft voice, as his hand slipped against Eben's cheek, tilting up his face. "You like it, then?"

Eben rapidly nodded, his breath escaping in a choked little gulp, his eyes now darting between Tryggr's flushed face, and the circlet of the *kraga* in his fingers. It was slim and elegant, its smooth gold brushed to a dazzling shine, broken only by a solid ring at the front for a chain. And as was the custom, there was text inscribed on the gold's inner edge, words that would never again be seen once the *kraga* was placed, fastened forever around an orc's throat, cradling his lifeblood within it.

And curse it, Eben couldn't even read the text through his blinking, leaking eyes, and Tryggr audibly swallowed, his thumb brushing away the streak of wetness on Eben's cheek. "It's got our vows written on it, too," he said, husky. "Saying how I want to keep you safe, and happy, for as long as I can. For—always. If you can put up with me that long, that is."

He'd huffed a hoarse, croaky little laugh, wryly shaking his head. And oh, oh, Eben couldn't bear it, not for another breath—and before he'd even caught it, he hurled himself forward, straight into Tryggr's arms. Clinging at him as tightly as he could, burying his face in his chest, as the sobs finally ripped out of his gasping, quivering throat.

"Yes," he choked. "Yes, Tryggr, yes, please. For—always. But are you sure—you cannot want—not a Ka-esh—what will your pa say, I—"

The sobs were breaking again, convulsing him in Tryggr's arms, but oh, those were Tryggr's warm hands, stroking him so steady, so certain. "I do want it," he said, quiet. "I've made up my mind, ach? You're so sweet, so soft and clever and generous and true. An' you're the best fuck I've ever had, and I miss you like hell when you're not around, and I—I can't bear the thought of losing you. So I'm not letting you get away. Not *ever*."

His voice cracked, his hands spasming against Eben's back,

his face pressing into Eben's hair. And that might even have been a sniff from his nose as he drew in breath, let it out. "An' as for Pa," he said, steadier, "he's not gonna say one damned word, until he's sorted out his mess with his mystery woman! He's gonna lose *Pabbi* over it if he don't shape up, and I'm not about to repeat his rubbish, ach? I found myself the sweetest Ka-esh in the realm to love and fuck and care for, so"—he drew back a little, twitched a wavering smile at Eben's wet face—"I'm gonna claim you as mine, and I'm gonna do it right. In the Skai ways, *and* the Ka-esh."

Eben still couldn't seem to breathe properly, the water streaking down his face, but he was still nodding, saying yes, yes, *yes*. Yes, he wanted this, he needed this, more than anything else he'd ever needed in his life. And he'd made up his own mind long ago, maybe even that first time he'd seen Tryggr in the corridor. *Looking for something, Ka-esh? Not lost, are you? I can show you the way...*

Tryggr was nodding too, giving Eben a fond, hopeful little smile, before pulling the *kraga* open on its hidden hinge, and holding it up before Eben's eyes. Letting him see what he'd be getting into, letting him read the lovely script of the traditional matehood vow inside it, etched forever in solid gold. *I grant you my sword, and my favour, and my fealty, so long as I am able, and so long as you shall wish.*

It was followed by both their names, *Tryggr of Clan Skai, and Eben of Clan Ka-esh.* And Eben's heart skipped as he read it, his breaths still shaky and ragged, his eyes blinking hard. His. *His.*

He couldn't have said who stepped forward first, him or Tryggr—but somehow the cool gold was touching his neck, circling close and careful around it. And Eben scarcely noticed Gareth stepping behind him, slipping a finger inside the solid gold ring, checking the fit before it was permanently latched. But it was perfect, it felt perfect, so perfect Eben felt dizzy all over with it. His *kraga*. *His.*

"Ach, this is good," came Gareth's distant voice behind him.

"Now you only need to fully close it, brother, and the bond shall be complete."

Eben shuddered all over, his eyes wide and beseeching on Tryggr's flushed face. And Tryggr nodded, his throat bobbing, as his hands shifted, and the gold circling Eben's neck snapped shut. Feeling so strong, so solid, like a steady certain hand holding safe around his throat. Like nothing Eben had ever imagined, and it was his, his, *forever.*

"You like it, ach?" Tryggr murmured, his eyes shifting with light and warmth, and oh, his hand was there too, skating against the feel of his gold around Eben's neck. "Feels good?"

Eben fervently nodded, his throat convulsing against that sweet brush of gold, while Tryggr's mouth twitched up, his dimple quivering in his cheek. "Ach, I ken," he murmured, as his other hand slipped down Eben's front, and groped at where he was somehow fully hard in his trousers. "Looks real good on you, too."

Eben gasped and jerked forward again, because he just needed to touch Tryggr, to hold him, anything, everything—when behind them, there was the sound of a polite cough. Right. Gareth.

Eben guiltily twisted around, a sheepish smile on his mouth—curse it, they hadn't even thanked him—but wait. Gareth was holding—something else. A thick gold bracelet, with a long, fine, glittering chain attached.

"You also wished for this part, did you not?" Gareth said, raising his brows toward Tryggr. "For you?"

There was a faint trace of a challenge in his voice, but Tryggr's grin toward him was only warm, grateful relief. "Ach, almost forgot," he replied, as he plucked the bracelet from Gareth's hand. "Thanks, brother."

Eben's bewilderment was rising again, because the bracelet looked like—no. Like it... *matched* the *kraga*, and it broke apart on a hinge, too. And inside it—inside it, again,

was that exact same script. The vow. Their names. As if...
as if...

"Thought it might not be—right, for a Skai to grant himself
a Ka-esh *kraga*," Tryggr said, in a rush. "But thought it might
still be more—fair, if I had aught to speak of our vow, too. An'
Gary had the idea of this, said you sometimes use 'em in the
dýflissa, so—"

He thrust the bracelet toward Eben with a sudden, jerky
movement, and Eben blinked down at it, and then up at
Tryggr's face. At where he again looked and scented nervous,
almost shy, glancing away like that, rubbing his hand at his
bound-back hair. "But only—if you wanna, though," he added,
too quickly. "Maybe I oughta talked to you first, made sure
you'd even—"

But somehow Eben's other hand had snapped out, and
circled around Tryggr's wrist. Feeling the rapid pulse of his
blood, the sweaty heat of his skin, the familiar muscles shifting,
tensing, and... softening. Relaxing. Wanting this, too. Wanting
it so much he'd gone and arranged it, he'd ordered it, he'd
given Eben yet another brilliant, wondrous gift.

"Of course I wish to," Eben said, soft, as the slow, genuine
smile drew up his mouth. "This was so generous of you, Tryggr.
Thank you."

Tryggr's cheeks reddened, his head slightly ducking, his
hand spasming in Eben's grip. And now it was Eben opening
the gold's hinge, and then carefully closing its solid strength
around Tryggr's wrist. Where it fit snugly enough that it
wouldn't fall off, but not so snug that it would affect his
mobility or circulation, either.

"You are sure?" Eben asked, searching Tryggr's own
blinking eyes. "You will not... regret this?"

Tryggr shook his head, rapid and decisive, so Eben drew in
a slow, shaky breath, and gently snapped the bracelet closed.
His bracelet, his gold, on Tryggr's wrist. *His*. And he couldn't

stop staring at it, his breath again hitching in his throat, his cock swelling even fuller in his trousers. His. Forever.

He could hear Tryggr's swallow, the choked little sniff—but when his eyes darted up again, Tryggr was smiling again, his lips only slightly quivering. "Now we match, ach?" he said. "An' now you'll never get away from me, pet."

Because oh, yes, there was still the chain, clipped to the other side of the bracelet, dangling toward the floor. A chain that had a clip on the other end, too, and more heat thudded to Eben's groin as Tryggr brought the chain up, and hooked it onto the ring at his own throat.

"There," Tryggr murmured, giving a gentle tug of the chain with his bracelet. "Gonna be a good, obedient little pet on your lead for me, aren't you?"

Fuck. Eben moaned and nodded, stroking his shaky hand down the fine gold chain. Feeling how strong it was, how beautifully crafted, and it was his. His lead. So his lord could keep him nearby, keep him safe, keep them bound together, make Eben do whatever the hell he wished...

And yes, Tryggr's eyes were flickering, simmering with hunger and satisfaction as his hand gently tugged the chain, and pulled Eben forward. Commanding him without a word, or a touch, and Eben moaned again, biting at his lip, tilting his head back. Fuck, this was good, this was going to be so damned good, he was already almost about to—

But behind Eben, there was another light, polite cough from Gareth, jolting Eben back to awareness again. They were still in the forge, Gareth was still here, and Gareth had wielded all his stunning skill to grant them this impossible gift.

"Thank you—so much, brother," Eben said, his voice catching as he spun toward Gareth, his hand on his heart. "This was—such a great, great kindness. Most of all after all else you have done for me."

Gareth waved it away, but his eyes were soft, his cheeks

slightly flushed. "Think naught of it," he said. "I am glad to see you so content."

Eben's eyes were prickling again, his smile wavering on his mouth—until there was a very light, but telling, tug on the chain at his throat. "Ach, thanks again, Gary," Tryggr said, as he stepped toward the door. "I'll bring you the rest of the coin tomorrow. An' mayhap"—he winked over his shoulder—"I'll see if I can't send Hallr down for another visit, too."

Gareth's eyes instantly brightened at the mention of Hallr, who Eben now knew was one of Tryggr's Skai clanmates—in fact, the one he'd been fucking that first day they'd met in the corridor. And Eben also knew that Gareth and Hallr had now had several very intense encounters in the *dýflissa*, the most recent of which had sent a bloody, limping Hallr to the sickroom. And according to Tryggr, Hallr had been both subdued and furious afterwards, making short, snide comments about arrogant overbearing Ka-esh, while also reeking of hunger whenever he caught Gareth's scent in the corridor.

It all boded well, to Eben's mind—if there was any Ka-esh who could settle a surly, high-strung Skai, it was Gareth. And Eben knew how much Gareth had enjoyed those encounters with Hallr, too, and how he'd scented of warmth and contentment for days afterwards. And when Hallr had been convalescing in the sickroom, Gareth had even regularly stopped by to visit, bringing him baskets of sweets, and scenting only of satisfaction when Hallr had sulked and glared at him in return.

And even now, Eben could taste the eagerness on Gareth's scent, the hot thread of his rising hunger as he gave Tryggr a curt, grateful nod. "Ach, I shall be glad to see him," he replied. "If he is brave enough to again face my whips, and my prick."

Tryggr barked an amused laugh, surely knowing exactly how Hallr would greet such a message, and waved goodbye as he tugged Eben toward the door. Again guiding him with only the chain, but it already felt... easy, somehow. Instinctive. Right.

And it felt right for Tryggr to guide Eben through the corridor like this, too. Leading him by the neck through the Ka-esh wing, past any number of Eben's clanmates and acquaintances. Some of whom looked jealous, some pleased, some surprised—and when Tristan and Salvi appeared up ahead, Salvi's steps actually faltered, his eyes darting guiltily toward Tristan's bare neck beside him.

"Congratulations, brother," Salvi belatedly told Eben, while Tristan warmly nodded beside him. "Just what you needed, ach?"

Eben shyly nodded back, his face heating, while beside him, Tryggr was smugly smiling, and giving the chain another gentle little tug. Pulling Eben away again, up through the mountain, past many more curious-looking friends and acquaintances. And the further they walked, the more triumphant Tryggr scented, especially once they'd entered the Skai wing. Where none other than Drafli strode around a corner, Alma's black cat curled around his shoulders—but there wasn't even a flicker of surprise in his eyes as he smoothly signed toward Tryggr.

Good work, he said. *Very pretty.*

Tryggr's grin back was broad and delighted, and he was still grinning as he guided Eben into their cozy, familiar room. Which now felt far smaller than it once had, what with the addition of a large, sturdy new desk and all Eben's books. But Tryggr hadn't seemed to mind, and he'd even been the one to order the desk, along with a matching bookshelf. And after watching Eben squinting at his books for multiple nights on end, Tryggr had even gotten him a lovely pair of human-made spectacles, which had proven remarkably helpful, and now always held a place of honour on the desk beside Eben's new notebook, ink, and quill. All of which had been mating-gifts from Tryggr's fathers, who had almost begun to treat Eben as if he was their son, too.

It had all made Eben feel so welcomed, so cherished, like he truly did belong here, in Tryggr's room, in Tryggr's life. And now he had Tryggr's *kraga*, Tryggr's chain—and oh, the way Tryggr was looking at him, smiling at him, and gently tugging him toward the bed. Pulling off their clothes as they went, until they were both bared and tumbling onto the fur together, Eben's arms and legs twining up around Tryggr's back, as Tryggr settled over him, and caught his mouth in his. Kissing him with soft, gentle sweetness as his bobbing cock found Eben's still-soft, still-wet hole, and slid slow and easy inside.

Eben moaned and arched and rocked to meet him, clutching his mate as tightly as he could. Revelling in the kiss of his mouth, the fullness of his cock, the strength of his lean body, the truth of his gold around his neck. And Tryggr had wrapped the gold chain around his hand as they'd kissed, so now he could draw Eben up by the neck, drink more of him, bite into his lip, plunder his mouth and his hole and his heart. Making Eben his, his, again and again, bound together with flesh and blood and gold and teeth.

"You like it, my perfect pet?" Tryggr gasped, ragged, into his mouth. "Wish for more?"

And in this moment, lost in the sweep and the sway, the bite of Tryggr's mouth, the steady grind of his hips, the longing in his scent, Eben didn't know if he meant the kissing, the ploughing, the *kraga*, the room, their life. Or maybe it was all of it, all of this warm whispering wonder, this pleasure, this peace, this impossible, unthinkable home. *Home.*

"Ach, yes," Eben whispered back, so full, so perfect he could burst. "Yes. Always. *More.*"

THE END

THANKS FOR READING!

Thank you so much for reading this novella! I've wanted to write Tryggr and Eben's story ever since they first showed up, and I'm so, so grateful to the generous members of my Orc Sworn Patreon for making it possible. Thank you!

It was so rewarding to write about an orc with a quieter, gentler personality, who struggled with the same things so many of us struggle with—low self-worth, comparison with others, oppressive expectations, shame over not measuring up. I loved that through his relationship with Tryggr, Eben learned to show himself compassion, and to value his own contributions. I really hope that even if we don't all have a loudmouth Skai fuckboy to teach us a few lessons, we can treat ourselves with that same compassion, and remember that our own desires, needs, and contributions are all worthy of good Skai care. ❤

Also, I'd like to send a heartfelt thank-you to all the friends, beta readers, and cultural consultants who made time for my last-minute "short story" (ha ha): Amy F., Anne-Marie, Ari, Erin, Kahaula, Lauren Mauchley, Lou M., Mary Lynne Nielsen, MK, Otto, Serena, and Þórey H. I'm also extremely grateful to Lillian Lark and V.C. Lancaster (who are both fabulous authors in this genre), for sharing their very helpful insights! And my deepest gratitude to the absolutely brilliant Eris Adderly, who is not only an incredible author herself, but also a true editing goddess. Her guidance on this book was such a huge help to me, and I am just so grateful!

I also want to mention the fierce friends who have so

generously shared their gifts with our entire Orc Sworn community. A massive thank-you to my faithful Right Hand Marykate for all the constant help and support; to Amy and Elizabeth, for helping to make my Discord such a fun and welcoming community; to Erin, fearless leader of the Skai Mafia PR Team, whose true Skai fealty has been such a gift; to our delightful Grisk galdr-spinner Morning Dove for the tales, kindness, and friendship; to Coco for the perfect character designs and illustrations; to EJ and the Skai sisters for the awesome Tales from the Orc Den podcast; to Katie at Romantically Inclined Reviews for all the laughter and enthu-siasm; and to all my reviewers and friends who help spread the Orc Sworn love!

And as always, my deepest thanks to my own fierce Skai mate, who's always here to back me up and throw his daggers. :)

Thank you again for being here, and sharing this story with me. I hope to see you at Orc Mountain again soon!

ALSO BY FINLEY FENN

YULED BY THE ORCS

"He is my gift to you, this Yule's Eve. Shall you accept this from me?"

In a world of orcs and powerful men, Lydia is a shy, widowed washerwoman, forgotten and alone—until the day the orc drops in, with a full sack of laundry on his back.

He's tall, rangy, and utterly confounding, with his silver hair, his deep jolly laugh, and his twinkling, coal-black eyes. And when he offers to bring Lydia great joy, it's a gift that just keeps giving, drawing her ever deeper into his wicked, wondrous charms...

At least, until he invites her to spend Yule's Eve at his cozy, candlelit cabin. And when Lydia arrives, he offers her a brand-new gift, wrapped in a pretty red bow...

Another orc.

A stranger.

For her... *merriment.*

And he's the biggest, most terrifying monster she's ever seen in her life.

Will Lydia refuse her hideous gift, and run alone into the cold winter's night? Or can she find joy with a monster... or maybe even a home?

ALSO BY FINLEY FENN

THE SINS OF THE ORC

He's fallen too far to save... but his enemy is going to try.

In a world of warring orcs and men, Kesst of Clan Ash-Kai is a pawn. A pretty, pliant plaything, bound to the cruelest orcs in the realm.

Until the new healer storms in.

He's huge, hostile, and hideous, with a powerful scarred body and terrifying ancient magic. And it only takes one disastrous meeting before he and Kesst are bitter enemies, and Kesst vows to see the vile brute destroyed...

And then a sudden, deadly attack hurls his helpless body straight at the healer's feet.

Kesst fully expects to be mocked, belittled, abandoned to his doom—but instead, his new enemy picks him up.

Soothes his wounds.

And carries him home...

Soon Kesst is trapped in a tiny sickroom beneath Orc Mountain, caught in the thrall of the healer's impossible magic. In the surprising gentleness of his touch. In the strength of his stubborn, seductive safety...

But with his horrid handlers close on their scent, Kesst can't possibly be falling for his forbidden foe... can he? Can a healer save him from his sins... or destroy him?

ABOUT THE AUTHOR

Finley Fenn is "the queen of dark orc romance" (Virgo Reader), and her ongoing Orc Sworn series has been praised as "sexy, romantic, angsty, and captivating ... utter brilliance" (Romantically Inclined Reviews).

When she's not obsessing over her stories, Finley loves reading, drooling over delicious orc artwork, and spending time with her incredible readers on Patreon, Discord, and Facebook. She lives in Canada with her beloved family, including her very own grumpy, gorgeous orc husband.

For free bonus stories and epilogues, special offers, and exclusive Orc Sworn artwork, sign up at www.finleyfenn.com.

www.ingramcontent.com/pod-product-compliance
Lightning Source LLC
Chambersburg PA
CBHW032306310726
48973CB00008B/2533